RAVE REVIEWS FOR FRED GROVE!

"This reviewer can tr... a
Grove book he didn't ...
—Ben T. Haywick, *The ...stone Epitaph*

"Grove is among the most honored Western writers in
America today."

—*Tucson Weekly*

"Grove has always been a master storyteller who keeps
his plots twisting but never losing focus of his characters."

—*The Shootist*

"Fred Grove knows how to add complications to a plot,
how to draw characters you care about, and how to describe the land like few other writers."

—*Roundup*

"A gripping, fast-paced historical novel...a must read."
—*Booklist* on *The Years of Fear*

IN THE SHADOW OF THE NOOSE

Before him, the hangman stood poised to loop the noose over Gabe's head, ever mindful of the hooting approval urging him on.

The hangman was Ike Cole. Gold teeth shining. Planter's hat at a rakish angle.

Jesse waved his six-shooter at him, shouting: "Stop it, Cole! That man works for me!"

Instead, Cole turned to Gabe with the noose.

At the same instant, Jesse saw that, if the two men released the horse just as Cole got the noose on, Gabe would hang.

"For the last time, stop this or I'll fire!" Jesse yelled at Cole.

Cole ignored him, almost taunting, tense, ready, waiting, standing on the balls of his feet. The lead horse, still fighting the bit, was forced closer. Gabe dodged quickly as Cole made a tentative try with the noose.

Jesse was going to shoot Cole when a slurred voice snarled in his ear: "You ain't gonna shoot nobody, Yankee!"

Jesse felt a swinging blow across his left shoulder that knocked him off balance, nearly to the ground. Simultaneously he heard the blast of a gun.

A SOLDIER RETURNS

FRED GROVE

LEISURE BOOKS   NEW YORK CITY

A LEISURE BOOK®

January 2007

Published by special arrangement with Golden West Literary Agency.

Dorchester Publishing Co., Inc.
200 Madison Avenue
New York, NY 10016

ISBN 0-8439-5812-X

Visit us on the web at www.dorchesterpub.com.

A SOLDIER
RETURNS

CHAPTER ONE

Jesse Wilder drew rein some distance from the house, smiling at the familiar scene in front. Gabe Jackson, that peerless ex-slave, was leading a burro carrying Jimmy and Jamie, hollering like demons. Susan Lattimore came out and waved as they passed on toward the corrals, the patient Gabe watching that the squirming pair did not fall off.

Somewhat solemnly Jesse felt the excitement here, the pure peace and happiness. Now a change was coming. It had to be met, and honored, because it was family, his family, which once had been solid and good.

Instead of unsaddling at the corrals, he rode up to the adobe house and looped the reins around a verandah post and went in. Better to tell Susan now.

She met him almost at the door, her eyes seeking why as she greeted him with a kiss. "You look very thoughtful," she said. "Something wrong?"

He showed her a letter. "My brother Claiborne has died of yellow fever . . . in New Orleans."

"Oh, Jesse!" she exclaimed, taking his arm.

"My sister, Mary Elizabeth Somerville, has written me . . . forwarded by B. L. Sawyer, the old family attorney." He grinned wryly. "The only friend I've had back there."

"I'm so sorry," she said, embracing him.

"Claiborne and I were never close . . . he was eleven years older, for one thing. We had different views. I was a liberal schoolteacher and could see changes looming ahead for the South and for us back there in Tennessee. He was educated as a lawyer and a red-hot Secessionist. He and my father were outraged when, with friends dying around me in Yankee prison, to save my own life I volunteered to serve in the Union Army out West. They felt I'd dishonored the family. Yet, I know that I always loved Claiborne as a brother."

"Did he serve in the Army?"

"He became a government purchasing agent in Atlanta with the rank of major. When Atlanta fell, he shifted to New Orleans. He didn't serve in the field, but I never begrudged him a safe job. We needed supplies." He paused, reluctant to go on. "There's much more to the letter. You read it."

"You tell me about it first," she said gently. "Then I'll read it."

He took her hand, and they went into a bright room that led to the patio and sat, facing each other. "Mary Elizabeth lives in Lexington, Kentucky," he began. "Happily married to a tobacco farmer. She's three years younger than I am . . . a mighty sweet girl. She used to write me and send me things. All that stopped in prison . . . nothing got through. If it did, the guards took it. . . . My mother had passed on before the war, and in his will my father left the farm to Claiborne and Mary Elizabeth. I found that out when I was mustered out after the war and went home, a pariah for sure. Everybody knew I'd worn the hated blue . . . old family friends turned their backs. Mister Sawyer wanted me to contest the will, but I said no. The farm was my father's to do as he wished. I say farm because it wasn't a plantation. My father bred and sold mules to cotton farmers in the deep South. We raised corn and hogs for our own use. Had a big orchard. It's a nice place. Mister Sawyer said Claiborne sold off all the stock."

He shook his head in an unbelieving way. "Now Mary Elizabeth says she will deed the farm to me, if I'll occupy it. Otherwise, she'll sell it. She writes that she is sad about what I've gone through and hopes, this way, she can help make up for what happened. She will meet me back there in Petersburg, if I'll agree."

Susan drew back and he saw fear sweep into her eyes.

"Not to move back and take over the farm," he quickly assured her. "Never . . . our home is here in Arizona, around Tucson. But I must go back and see her. At long last a coming together of the family I'd given up on years ago."

They were suddenly quite close. "I understand how you feel, Jesse. Yes, you must go back and see your only sister . . . bring your family together again. But you're not going alone. We're all going . . . all the family."

"Why, yes! Why not?"

He regarded her with unbounded appreciation, this dark-haired woman with warm blue-green eyes, this loving woman who he could not yet marry because Rutherford Lattimore of Philadelphia would not agree to a divorce, instead choosing to delay and accuse her of abandonment and adultery, and Jesse with alienation of affection.

"I knew you would understand," he said, putting his arms around her.

"I'm also afraid what Rutherford will do when we go back there."

"Nobody's going to harm you and Jimmy," he said firmly.

"I mean what he can do through the courts. He can be a very ruthless man. He's very ambitious, expects to be elected a U.S. senator this fall."

Jesse's mind flashed back to when the volunteers had returned to Tucson. Rutherford Lattimore had been waiting at the hotel, a bearded man of patrician bearing, stern of face, inflexible. Both Susan and Jesse had tried to explain the struggle to rescue Jimmy, the cost in men's lives. But Lattimore had seemed mainly concerned with her in the company of "uncouth frontier characters."

"You and Jimmy are going home with me on the next eastbound!" he had shouted, ready to strike her.

Jesse had stepped between them. No, they were staying here with him. He loved them and would care for them. In that moment he had seen much more revealed. Jimmy feared his stepfather. And Lattimore had struck Susan in the past.

Lattimore had turned and walked away when Susan had informed him they were staying. But Jesse knew the fight to gain her freedom had just begun.

After a little run of silence, Jesse, to comfort her, said: "There's another way to look at going back. It's the only way to get this settled. We can't do it from here . . . he'll put off and delay . . . anything to hurt you. It's been months now. I'll get B. L. Sawyer to represent us. My father said he was the best country lawyer in middle Tennessee. Tough in the courtroom. He knows the law."

"It frightens me, Jesse. I hate to leave the blessed peace and happiness we've all had out here."

"I know. I do, too. But you can't hold back after all you've been through . . . hiring volunteers to rescue Jimmy from Juh's Apaches. And, incidentally, Jamie, too. Then the running fight from the Burro Mountains almost to Fort Bowie. And, just when we thought we were in the clear on the way back, the Army deserters trying to take over and you shooting the ringleader. I've never seen a braver thing, Susan."

Just then the boys came romping in, tugging on each other, followed by the smiling Gabe.

"Uncle Gabe's gonna make us bows and arrows," Jimmy gushed. "Take us rabbit huntin'."

"If you're good," Gabe cautioned, shaking a finger. "And remember to feed de burro."

"Oh, we will, won't we, Jamie?"

"We b-be goo-boys," Jamie said, jumping up and down.

Juh's Apaches had wiped out Jamie's family on the Mimbres River in New Mexico; apparently they had held him about two years when, in an unusual twist of events, a gift horse for Juh and later a raid on Juh's camp, he was freed with Jimmy, who had been taken captive for a short time after a stagecoach was attacked with him and his doomed uncle among the passengers.

The horror of what Jamie had witnessed still

haunted him sometimes at night, and he would cry out. His speech also had been affected at times, leaving him halted and searching for words. Out of his tangled thoughts Susan and Jesse had decided Jamie was his given name, and soon he began to respond to it. Susan had become the loving, comforting mother he needed. He and Jimmy were like brothers, constantly wrestling, teasing, disagreeing, making up, running, playing games. Both were blue-eyed and fair-haired, except Jamie's hair was a pale yellow.

Susan had instructed Jimmy: "You are older than Jamie and must be a brother and protect him. Do not talk about what happened to his folks in New Mexico, unless he says something. Be generous. Share what you have. Don't be selfish. Remember, he's had very little. If you see him being sad, put your arm around him and call him brother. You will do that, won't you?"

"Yes, Mama," Jimmy had said, and saluted, sealing his promise.

"Gabe, we have news for you," Susan said. "We're all going back to Tennessee so Jesse can see the sister he hasn't seen in years. Do you want to go with us? You are welcome. As we've said before, we think of you as part of the family."

Gabe smiled at her words. A runaway slave from Alabama before the Civil War, he was neither servile nor arrogant. At peace with himself and all around him. He stood a good six-two, strong and straight, with the bearing of a free man who had made his own way despite many difficulties and the prejudice of a hostile world. The boys loved him. He had endless patience and was constantly thinking up ways to entertain them.

Gabe Jackson could read!

He had related that with evident pride when he volunteered to go on the mission led by Jesse to rescue Jimmy. "Ah took care a broken-down, sweet ol' bachelor preacher in New Awlins fo' a long time. We prayed together ever' day. An he teached me to read, he did, that sweet ol' man. It was like a big door swingin' open an' de golden light streamin' through. Oh, my, it was wonderful!" Before the sweet old man died, he had given Gabe a treasured Bible, which he still read daily. Besides knowing how to handle mules, Gabe had said he could go days without food or water. Had many times. And, spoken with pride, he told them he would make "the bes' co'nbread you evah tasted. An' biscuits, too. Ah kin cook anything. Clean game."

He did some of the cooking now, which he enjoyed, but wasn't treated as a servant. Jesse and Susan had offered to stake him if he wished to try his luck in California. But Gabe had declined, saying he'd rather stay with "home folks" and work for them, if they wanted him to. They had assured him that they did and that there would always be a place for him. Furthermore, Jesse had plans to furnish stock for the stages and freight lines hauling to the mines. And he would need a good man to handle mules in the cotton fields.

Now, Gabe was silent so long about going with them that Jesse said: "You could stay here and take care of the place. It's up to you."

"Tennessee," Gabe said, considering, "that's a slave state."

"Not anymore. Not since the war. You'd have nothing to fear."

"You know, Mistuh Jesse, a man that's been a slave nevah gits ovah all that feelin'. It's like he was branded. An' goin' back theah, Ah know Ah'd be lookin' ovah my shoulder."

"But you're a free man, Gabe. The war's long over. Your freedom can't be taken from you." He looked intently at Gabe. "Have you had any trouble in town? Has anybody said anything?"

Gabe shook his head. "Jest a few looks from white men passin' through on West. Like, what was Ah doin' out here?"

"They could be asked the same question. But if you'd feel uneasy back there, maybe you'd better stay here."

"Ah have done decided," Gabe said suddenly, breaking into a smile, his eyes taking them all in. "Ah'll go with de family."

"*Your* family," Jesse said, images vivid in his memory of Gabe's riding back and forth, shielding Susan and the boys during the desperate fight to reach Fort Bowie.

And by then the boys were jumping up and down, voicing approval.

CHAPTER TWO

Entering the town square of Petersburg, Jesse could feel the onrush of mingled feelings, for this had been his home town. First of all he thought of his dear departed mother, and then of his boyhood friends, none of whom had survived the war, forever leaving him with a sense of guilt for having lived through it. Here they had all volunteered that day, while the band played "The Bonnie Blue Flag" and "Dixie" as the ever-smiling girls watched and waved, some weeping.

He took the first turn off the square and halted the team of mules drawing the rented Dougherty wagon. Covered like an Army ambulance, only better, it had side doors entered via a hanging iron step plate, transverse seats like a stagecoach, canvas side curtains which could be rolled up or strapped down, and in back a chain-supported boot for baggage. By far the most comfortable and convenient way for a family of five to travel with considerable belongings and food. To the boys' delight, they had camped out two nights coming down from Nashville.

Leaving the boys with Gabe, Jesse escorted Susan across the street and down a short way to B.L. Sawyer's office, hoping to find him in.

The same officious, middle-aged secretary with the stony expression was there, and, Jesse thought, posted like a sentry guarding the palace gates.

"I'm Jesse Wilder," he informed her. "With me is Missus Susan Lattimore. I wrote Mister Sawyer not long ago that we would be coming in from Arizona to see him on various family matters. Just wanted to stop by and greet him today."

The firm features relaxed a trifle, no more. "Mister Sawyer received your letter, Mister Wilder. He's very busy, as usual. I'll see if he has time today."

Jesse felt like smiling. She was merely doing her job. But why did she have to act so regally, as if granting him an audience with Petersburg's leading attorney?

She went to a closed door, rapped discreetly, and after a short wait entered, quietly easing shut the door behind her.

Within a few moments, a ringing voice exclaimed: "Jesse Wilder! Show them in at once, Miss Pringle!"

Her set features approaching the breaking point of graciousness as she came out, Miss Pringle said softly—"Mister Sawyer will see you now."—at the same time giving Susan an up-and-down appraisal.

Jesse thanked her and escorted Susan in.

Sawyer appeared even more gaunt and gray than on that down day in this room, when with evident regret he had read the provisions of Thomas H.

Wilder's will to Jesse, come home after being mustered out of Union Army of the West. But he stood quite erect despite his seventy-some years. With head held high and his handsome white beard close cropped, he projected dignity and forthrightness to go with the lively benign eyes and courtroom voice. Too old for active duty in the war, he had captained a county company of militia that had seen only the dust of a few Yankee cavalry scouts.

He not only grasped Jesse's hand, he then clapped him on the shoulder. "I'm very glad to see you, Jesse. You look much better than when I last saw you."

"Very pleased to see you, sir."

Introductions quickly made, Sawyer bowed and gestured to chairs in front of his long desk.

"In his last letter about coming back," Sawyer said, smiling at Susan, "he told me much about you, Missus Lattimore, and I can see that he didn't exaggerate one bit."

"Oh, my," she said, a bit flustered. "Jesse is very kind, and we have been through a great deal together. I feel most fortunate and blessed because of him."

"He also wrote at length how you rode on the mission with the volunteers into the mountains in hopes of rescuing your young son Jimmy, which was accomplished."

"At a very high cost," she said in a low voice. "We lost some good men. I often think of how they sacrificed their lives so I could have my son back. In doing that, another boy was freed. I'll never forget what they did."

"Which we Southerners can well understand. Not

far from here was the Battle of Franklin, which some refer to as our Gettysburg of the West. Historians will be studying it a hundred years from now and ever more, asking why General Hood spent his men so recklessly."

"We stopped there on the way down and went over the battlefield," Jesse said. "I showed Susan the embattled Carter House, and about where I was knocked out of the war. It took me back."

A respectful silence seemed to settle over the room. As if in a reminiscent mood, Sawyer said: "Tennessee lost so many fine young men there, the entire state was plunged into mourning. In Franklin, every house, church, school, and public building was turned into a hospital." Then, in a considerate manner to Susan: "Didn't mean to get off so much on the war, but we've all felt its effects and will for a long time, in many ways."

Jesse said: "In that respect, sir, I should tell you that Susan lost Jimmy's father, Lieutenant James Bryant of the Union Army, at First Bull Run."

Sawyer straightened, looking at Susan in surprise, his expression softening. "You have my very deepest sympathy, Missus Lattimore. I mean that. I just hate to hear it."

"Thank you, Mister Sawyer."

To ease the moment, he smiled his encouragement at her, saying: "And you have named your boy after his father?"

"And my father," she said.

He nodded instant approval. "I like the idea of carrying on family names, though when it gets down to the third or the fourth, I draw the line. Sounds like royalty. Instead, why not make it the middle name? Naturally, I'm an authority, since I have no sons. I say that with regret," he concluded, smiling at Susan.

Their conversation had placed them all at ease, and now he regarded them together, as a counselor would, sensing there was much left untold and to go over, waiting.

"Now that we're here," Jesse said, "I'll write Mary Elizabeth. She said she'd come down. I am looking forward to seeing her after all these years. We always got along."

"Did you make it clear to her that you won't take the farm?"

"Yes, sir. She said if I didn't, she would put it on the market. I have to say I am sad to see it go out of the family. But Susan's life and mine have changed, and we have made our home in Arizona."

"As a matter of fact, Jesse, Claiborne put it up for sale immediately after your father died. But he's had it priced too high for these times. It's going to take a long while before we get back to where we were before the war."

"I suppose Claiborne's had someone on the place?"

"Farming on shares. They come and go. You know how that can be? It's hard to find reliable people now. But I fear I'm being unfair when I say that . . . with families uprooted by all that's happened. You'd be surprised at the number of people over the South moving out West to start over again . . . often to Texas." He made a gesture of self-reproach. "Well, you didn't come all this way to hear an old man lecture on the changing state of things."

"We're interested in whatever you have to say," Jesse assured him, and Susan nodded. "I've been out of touch for a long time. I feel like a stranger."

Sawyer smiled. "Well, getting back to the farm, Mary Elizabeth has a caretaker living there to look after things. A man I found for her . . . Silas Kemp, a widower. Served under General Cleburne. Survived Franklin. Wounded in Hood's last reckless onslaught at Nashville. Considered a good man."

"I'd think so after all that," Jesse said.

Sawyer pursed his lips, looked off and back, frowning. "I don't quite know how to say this. Don't want to make it sound more of a threat to the public peace than it is. . . . As if things weren't bad enough, we have night riders in our vicinity and around. Some small farmers have sold out and left. Frightened blacks have left for the cities."

Jesse stared at him. "Night riders?"

"No less, and they wear white robes. It appears that we have the Klan with us."

"The Klan? That's new to me."

"You've been gone. It was new to many of us until the last year or so. It's known as the Ku Klux Klan. A secret society organized after the war, they say, to reassert white supremacy. Seems to have first taken root around Memphis, then spread from there. They terrorize any black man who stands up for his rights . . . including any white man that gets in their way for a variety of reasons. In Giles County, the story goes, they decided to enforce their idea of public morals, by flogging a man rumored to be chasing another man's wife." He loosened a smile. "Guess our morals pass muster. So far just night riders in white robes to scare folks off their farms. I'm repeating what is common knowledge. Not living in the country, I've never seen them."

Jesse kept shaking his head.

"The South still has men who won't accept the fact that we lost the war," Sawyer said.

"Maybe the same ones that helped start it. And you say some people have sold out . . . left?"

"Yes. By intimidation . . . dashing by at night . . . shooting at houses. Sometimes nailing a note to a post to get out. So far no killings. But a great potential. All this adds to the general low economic situation we're in."

"What about the sheriff? Found out anything?"

"He's been called in more than once. But there's no trace of who's doing this."

"Who's buying up the farms?"

"In the first place, it doesn't take any capital to buy a farm discounted by fear. Only one I know of has been purchased by Mister Hanover."

Yancey Hanover, Jesse remembered. *Had the General Store.*

"A farmer I've known for years offered me his place for a song. At my age what would I do with a farm? I told him no. I didn't want to take advantage of a man who might regret later he'd given in to fear and sold out. . . . I understand an out-of-town banker has bought most of the farms, using some local man. Banker up at Lewisburg. Buy cheap and sell high. Someday times will get better and he'll stand to reap a big profit."

Silence grew, Jesse feeling a dull anger, finding it difficult to think of his home torn by violence and fear, people leaving. It had always been so peaceful around Petersburg. But there were still vital matters to be brought up today, and Mr. Sawyer was waiting. With a glance at Susan, he turned and said: "During the rescue mission, Susan and I found that we love each other very much. I won't go into all that happened, just how we got the boys, then a fighting retreat to Fort Bowie. . . . But unknown to us, three of the volunteers were Army deserters at Fort Bliss, Texas. After we left Bowie, they decided to take over, bent on doing some dreadful things . . . shot one of our best men. Had us all covered, but Susan. She shot the ringleader twice with her Army Colt . . . dead center . . . saved us all. . . . I should explain that she was well brought up. Her father was a Union cavalry officer. Taught her to ride and handle side arms."

Sawyer, eyes wide, broke into vigorous applause and gave out a passionate: "Wonderful! I am proud again to know you, Missus Lattimore! Indeed, I am, brave lady." He was smiling at her.

Susan was embarrassed and looked at Jesse with disapproval. "You shouldn't be telling that."

"On the contrary, it should be told," Sawyer insisted. "Like all brave deeds."

"I agree," Jesse said with a grin. "Susan herself would never tell it. The story of the mission would be incomplete without it." He paused to arrange his thoughts, thinking to tell it straight out, and said: "When we returned to Tucson, Susan's husband, Rutherford Lattimore, had arrived from Philadelphia a few days before. Instead of rushing to greet Susan and Jimmy, he confronted her. I saw that Jimmy feared his stepfather. Susan tried to explain what had taken place, and I tried. He refused to listen. Instead of showing relief and joy over Jimmy's rescue, he was furious at Susan for going with what he called *uncouth frontier characters*. When I saw that things were about to get out of hand, I stepped in. I said I loved them, and they were staying with me. He was struck dumb with astonishment . . . couldn't believe it. Then he asked Susan. When she told him yes, he said no more, just turned and left us. But I knew we were in for a long and nasty legal fight. We want you to represent us, Mister Sawyer. We want to get married as soon as we can, legally. We've been mighty happy these past months with our family."

"How far has this gone?"

"Susan wrote, asking for an amicable divorce. He was furious and refused and gave vent to his anger. I won't repeat all that he said. In short, he claimed abandonment and adultery, and me with alienation of affection."

"Beyond his letter of refusal, how far has he taken this?"

"There it stands."

"Let's see," Sawyer mused. "Arizona is a territory?"

"Yes. And Tucson is a village."

"And Rutherford Lattimore is in Philadelphia?"

Jesse nodded.

"I think this is mainly a threat at this time," Susan said.

"Anything to delay and cause Susan unhappiness," Jesse said. "We realized we'd have to come East to settle it, as much as we dread to get in a court fight."

"You may have to go to Philadelphia, unless you can reach an agreement through correspondence. But, first, will I represent you? Yes. Glad to, if you want an old-fashioned country lawyer?"

"We'd have no other," Jesse assured him. "My father said you were the best lawyer in middle Tennessee."

Sawyer let a half smile play across his face. "Old friends tend to exaggerate. I represented your father several times on stock matters and won for him. We pretty much agreed on everything except the provisions of his will. I wanted you to share equally. But—"

"I appreciated that. The will hurt because it meant what had been a close family when my mother lived was gone forever." Jesse lightened his tone, saying quickly: "As heavy as your practice is, sir, we realize it is mighty generous of you to take our case."

"Oh, yes," said Susan.

Sawyer leaned back and gazed unseeingly about, and then at them with a kind of gentle recalling. "I've reached the age and the stage when I can choose my cases. If farmer Brown's cows break into his neighbor's cornfield and there's the devil to pay, I shuffle the matter on to an enterprising young lawyer . . . just as such was passed on to me when I was starting out. Maybe I'd be paid five dollars, or with a ham or chickens or produce, which, as a struggling young lawyer, I was glad to get. But today I still would not turn away any deserving person in need of counsel, as I believe you do."

"Which we appreciate very much," Jesse said.

"To begin with," Sawyer said, facing Susan, "why do you think your husband's refusal is mainly just a threat at this particular time?"

"Rutherford is running for the U.S. Senate. As a prominent attorney in the public eye with big political ambitions, he's always been very careful about how he is perceived. Any hint of scandal would be disastrous."

"All the more reason for him to agree to parting without a fight. That wouldn't hurt him politically."

"But he won't agree. I know him. He wants to hurt me. So he'll delay and evade at least until after the election. Maybe longer, if elected."

Sawyer's jaw firmed. "We'll see about that. Now let's go back and you fill me in on your family troubles and how they started."

"First of all," she said slowly, "I am not without cause." She paused in thought, then: "Over two years ago I realized the need for Jimmy to have a father as he grew up. By that time, too, my father had passed on. He'd been so good to Jimmy. . . . I met Rutherford and hoped that the marriage would work out. It didn't. I soon learned that as a stepfather he had little or no patience and understanding for a lively boy not his own."

She fell silent, as if averse to bring up the unpleasant past.

"Perhaps we'd better discuss this later, when you've had time to rest up from your long trip?"

"Thank you, Mister Sawyer, but I must get on with it. You see, I'm not against spanking a child, if needed, but Rutherford thrashed Jimmy. It was close to a beating. We had words. When he started to do it again some days later, I stopped him . . . more words. Then he struck me. Mistakenly I thought at first I should bear it for Jimmy's sake, and maybe we could talk and patch things up. When he struck me again during an argument, twice, I took Jimmy and moved out of the house. . . . I have money that my father left me. . . . When Rutherford came on bended knee, I decided to try it once more. For a while there was peace . . . an uneasy peace at best."

After a short silence, she went on. "Just then my Uncle Tom Andrews, who had shipping interests on the West Coast, was getting ready to go by stage from St. Louis to San Diego. I saw a chance to get Jimmy out of the house. Could he go along? Uncle Tom was delighted. It would be a great adventure for a seven-year-old boy. He said there would be cavalry escorts all the way. But Apaches attacked the stage in New Mexico. Uncle Tom and all but one of the escort troopers were killed. The wounded survivor told what happened, next day, to a large party of travelers coming through. Jimmy had been taken captive."

Sawyer, an intense listener, asked: "How did you know where to get in touch with Jesse after all he's done? Into Mexico to aid the *Juáristas* fighting Maximilian, back to New Mexico and over into Arizona and down into Mexico again? He would always write me, telling me where he was going. There would be long gaps of silence. I would wonder about him, mixed with worry, then here would come a letter. How in the world did you ever find him?"

"Fortunately at that time he had been written up at length in the Philadelphia *Inquirer*, even in New York. The post commander at Fort Cummings was a correspondent. He aspired to write a history on President Juárez's victory in Mexico, showing how ex-Confederates had assisted with training and leadership. He interviewed Jesse, who was still there, when a gang of outlaws seized the commander's young son and held him for ransom at a mountain hideout. . . . Jesse rode with an advance detail of the rescue force that actually freed the boy during the main attack. All that was told in great detail by the grateful commander in the *Inquirer*. When I read it, I sensed that I had to find this Captain Jesse Alden Wilder, the man who had helped bring back a captive boy."

Sawyer held his marveling gaze on her. "What then?"

"Accompanied by the family lawyer, I headed West. We stopped at Fort Cummings and were told Captain Wilder had left for Arizona some time ago. At Fort Bowie, Arizona, we learned he'd gone to Tucson . . . after service as a scout on a secret government mission that freed the daughter of the governor of Sonora held by *bandidos*."

Her voice fell, ceased, and she seemed to relive what she was about to relate next. "I could hardly believe my good luck when I found that Jesse was at the very hotel where the stage stopped. And, soon, when at last I saw him, I told him that I thought God alone had led me to him. . . . I still believe that, Mister Sawyer."

He regarded her with gentle understanding. "Sometimes wonderful things happen for which we mere mortals can find no easy explanation. It is beyond us, because it's supposed to be. So we say our humble prayer of thanks and go gratefully on, filled with wonder."

They all sat a while in contemplative silence.

After working out the details regarding the letter Sawyer was to write to Rutherford Lattimore, and where, and Sawyer's insistence that they tell him more about what happened on the rescue mission, it was finally time to leave.

"We thank you again, sir," Jesse said. "We'll stay at the old home place. I hope Silas Kemp won't feel put out. He should like a change of cooking. We come well provisioned in a Dougherty wagon."

The men shook hands, and Susan hugged Sawyer and kissed his bearded cheek.

Watching them cross the street, hand in hand, Sawyer commented to Miss Pringle: "What those two have been through is almost beyond belief. Now, I'm going to get her a divorce from the meanest man in Philadelphia so she can marry the one she loves. Her husband is none other than the well-known corporation attorney, Rutherford Lattimore. Right now he's all bluster and threats. Meanwhile, he has big political ambitions . . . the U.S. Senate, no less. *Hmmn*. Well, the South may have lost the War Between the States, but we've still got a few shots left. Can you imagine, a brute of a man striking a woman with his fists! Prepare to take a letter, Miss Pringle," he concluded, and wheeled into his office.

CHAPTER THREE

"We're going out to the farm to stay a while," Jesse announced to the two young boys. "Out where I grew up. Have they worn you out, Gabe?"

"Ah made sandwiches, an dey went to sleep. When dey woke up, Ah tol' 'em a long story."

"About a great big ol' bullfrog," Jimmy spoke up, touching Jesse's arm. "He kept growin' an' growin'. He got so big that, when he jumped, Uncle Gabe said he splashed all the water outta the Mississippi River, he did."

"That *was* a big ol' bullfrog."

"But pretty soon it rained, an' the river filled up again."

"It sure did. Because, remember, we crossed the Mississippi at New Orleans, where we got on the steamboat?"

"I remember."

"Dey keep wonderin' where de mountains are," Gabe filled in.

"Well, boys," Jesse said, "where we're going, you'll

see some big hills that were my mountains when I was a boy."

Yancey Hanover, standing in front of his general store, watched with obvious curiosity as they passed at a trot. Other heads along the streets also were turning. *Not because a Dougherty wagon alone is such an unusual sight here,* Jesse thought bitterly. *It's because that's Jesse Alden Wilder, the notorious pariah who disgraced the South and a good family name by serving in the Union Army out West. What could bring him back? Well, he'll get nothing from me!*

Town Marshal Nate Burdette, still bulging with self-importance, left the Southland Saloon, and stood watching, rock-hard jaw thrust out, preening his handlebar mustache with a forefinger. An over-size star adorned his leather vest. A big pistol hung low on a broad belt. A long-ago scene, ludicrous at the time, rolled through Jesse's mind: *Burdette rushing out into the street and halting Jesse on his father's saddle horse, shouting:*

"You're gallopin' that horse! Violatin' a city ordinance. Went plumb around the square."

"I beg your pardon, sir. I was going at a fast trot."

"Reckon I know when a horse is on the gallop. That fast . . . might break loose and run over folks."

"In all due respect, Marshal. It was not a gallop."

"Don't argue with me, young sprout! It was a gallop and you are hereby fined five dollars. Pay the justice of peace."

"What are you grinning about?" Susan asked.

"That man we just passed is the town marshal of many years. He arrested me one time. Said I had galloped a horse around the square. I said it was a fast trot. I lost. He fined me five dollars. My father was furious with me. I had to borrow the money from him and work it out."

"Looking back," she teased, sitting closer to him, "would you still say it was a fast trot?"

"Why, Susan," he exclaimed, as if aggrieved, "would a pink-cheeked country lad, who always stood straight and true, have said no if it wasn't?"

"I had to wonder just a little, because I've seen you ride. You ride at a gallop more than you trot."

The chattering boys soon settled down, looking off and pointing, and by the time Jesse turned the mule team onto the pike, all his passengers seemed to share his silence. Before long the wooded hills would start changing colors. A kind of humble reverence and gratitude stole over him. So much had happened back then with family and friends. His parents' pride in him as an honor graduate of the Nashville Academy, and when the school board had unanimously chosen him over several others for the teaching position at Lost Creek. He had taught there until the country had gone mad, stuffed with hot pride and tinderbox outrage, spurred on by fire-eaters who could start a war but didn't know how to rein in the runaway hell they'd unleashed on others.

Today with Mr. Sawyer had brought back what once had been taken for granted here as a way of life: friendship, understanding, generosity. A day of restoration and faith. Feelings in the open. Susan made happy and hopeful. Now they could fight Rutherford Lattimore. Confronting the man as he had that day in Tucson, glimpsing his cruelty bared, Jesse knew that he would not free Susan without every mean-spirited means being tried against them. In all likelihood they would have to go to Philadelphia. There the battle would be fought. Thank God for a friend like B. L. Sawyer.

A familiar road that looked seldom traveled angled down from the low hills on his right and he turned that way, feeling more dread than expectation at what lay ahead.

"It's not far now," he said.

Susan looked at him, as if expecting him to say more, to show anticipation. He smiled at her, giving a little shake of his head, no more. *How different*, he thought, *this coming home is from the day I rode horseback out here expecting to find Father. Instead, finding the house boarded up. I knew then I was too late. I hope Silas Kemp is a fairly friendly sort. He must know my story. Everybody in the county must know it by now. Disgrace travels fast. Makes choice gossip. At least, Kemp and I share the common experience of having survived Franklin. Well, I made no apologies that day I returned and I won't now.*

He drove to a narrow lane and turned in slowly, by habit looking for sign, noting the recent broad tracks of a wagon. He continued on to a cluster of low sheds and corrals, a sagging barn turned a rusty brown, and a long corncrib with slatted sides like ribs. Everything rose behind a rail fence. He pulled up.

"My father bred and raised a lot of good cotton mules here," Jesse said. "Until the war, there was always a steady cash market in Mississippi and Alabama. Gabe, I believe you said you'd worked cotton mules."

"Ah did, in Alabama. Worked uh world of 'em. An' sometimes dey worked Gabe, contrary as mules kin be."

Jesse had to laugh. "Were you ever kicked by a mule?"

"Mo' times den Ah like to tell, befo' Ah smartened up."

"Uncle Gabe, where did the mule kick you?" ever-curious Jimmy wanted to know.

"Yes-sh, Uncle Gabe?" Jamie joined in.

Gabe shook his instructive finger at the pair. "Where Ah got kicked Ah just tol' de doctah, if dey was one. Mos' times de was no doctah in dem days."

"You mean it was a secret?" Jimmy persisted.

Gabe gazed off with a shrug, leaving the boys to ponder.

Jesse drove on, smiling to himself. Gabe knew just what to say or not to say.

The roomy old house of many memories took shape, stone chimneys rising like towers of strength at each end. The homey old place was not a decrepit relic of the past, Jesse thought, but stood there as a resolute reminder of enduring family ties of the busy past and not forgotten. It looked lived in. The window drapes were open. The yard had been raked. Not a piece was missing from the white picket fence, which looked recently painted. A rocker rested on the long front porch. Seeing all that, he felt a surge of pleasure.

Jesse halted the team and called out—"Hellooo-o-o, Mister Kemp! Helloo-o-o, Mister Kemp!"—preferring the courtesy of a greeting before everybody piled out on the man.

No one answered.

"Maybe he's out behind the house," Jesse said to Susan after a bit. "I'll go see. Everybody stay in the wagon."

He was striding that way when a lanky man came around the corner of the house. He walked with a limp. He slowed step, his bearded face forming a re-served greeting. He still wore a much-battered gray hat of the sort Jesse remembered that enlisted men had liked, low, flat-crowned, with a wide brim. A marching man had to have a hat.

"I'm Jesse Wilder," he said, holding out his hand. "Missus Mary Elizabeth Somerville's brother. I take it, you're Mister Kemp?"

"Yes . . . Silas Kemp. Heard you call." He spoke with a slow, soft voice and took Jesse's hand briefly. There seemed to be a decided distance about his manner, yet he was courteous. "Missus Somerville did write that you folks would be coming."

"Only for a while," Jesse said. "Mainly to see her and tend to some family matters. My home is in Ari-zona, where I'll be going back with my family." He left it there, hoping that made it clear he had no intention of leaving Kemp without a place to live. "We came pretty well provisioned, Mister Kemp. And we'd like for you to take your meals with us, if it's convenient?"

Surprise broke the rather inscrutable cast of Kemp's face. The black eyes under the bushy brows grew warmer. "Why, thank you, Mister Wilder. I shore would, and I am much obliged to you. Been batchin' since my wife passed away last year."

"I am sorry to hear that. Mister Sawyer told us. He also said that you served under General Cleburne."

"Yes, suh."

"No more need be said. My day there ended around the Carter House. When I came to, I was in a Yankee hospital in Nashville. You've probably heard the rest of the story more than once? I'm sure it's generally known."

Kemp offered no reply. He had spoken in a matter-of-fact way, without a trace of bitterness. He would not complain before any veteran who had survived Franklin.

"I want you to meet my family," Jesse said then, and, walking back, waved for everyone to get out.

As he introduced all the family, including Gabe Jackson, Susan at once offered a gracious hand to Kemp, who swept off his hat.

"I've invited Mister Kemp to have his meals with us," Jesse said. He had made the invitation on impulse.

"Oh, yes," Susan said as if she had known in advance. "You are, indeed, welcome, Mister Kemp. Our pleasure."

"I do thank you folks."

"We hope we don't inconvenience you or disturb you in any way," she said earnestly. "Jimmy and Jamie get pretty lively at times."

"Glad to have the company. It's been just me and the hoot owls."

"Jesse is so looking forward to seeing Mary Elizabeth again. Then we'll be going on."

Gabe Jackson had stayed by the mules during the introductions, he and Kemp exchanging nods. Two proud men. This was still the South, Jesse thought, and change would come very slowly. Although slavery was out, equality was not yet waiting in the wings. Kemp had not offered his hand and would

not be expected to here. Certainly a black man
would not unless the white man did. Even so, Jesse
was glad that he had pushed the bounds of propriety a little.

"Well," Kemp said, apologetic, "I'd better show
you-all the house now. I've slept downstairs. It
won't be just as you remember it, Mister Wilder.
Some wear and tear on the furniture. Folks movin'
in and out. Some not used to nice things."

Jesse felt a wave of memories engulf him as they
entered the musty-smelling house. His steps
sounded extra loud on the hardwood floor of the
hallway. It gave him a pang when he saw the deep
scratches on his mother's cherished oak dining
room table. The heavy cane-backed chairs looked
equally hard-used, but not broken. His mother's
cherry-wood hutch stood staunchly by, one drawer
sagging.

"Some folks don't have much bringin' up," Kemp
commented futilely, trying to close the drawer.

They came to the office, cramped with a burdened
wooden filing cabinet standing askew amid neatly
stacked red ledgers and farm journals on tables,
everything pretty much as Jesse remembered his or-
derly father had kept it, including the writing desk
with pen and inkhorn.

In the parlor Jesse noted the faded window drapes
and the familiar claw-footed tea table and the wing
chair, which his father had liked, and the now down-
trodden horsehair sofa, which he remembered his
mother had ordered shipped in from Nashville. Going on, he noted one feature that hadn't changed, the
rugged limestone fireplace in the living room.

"I've been gettin' in some firewood in case I'm still here when cold weather comes," Kemp said.

"I hope you are," Jesse said. He liked the soft-spoken Johnny Reb, felt an undeniable kinship of survival. His impulse strengthened to urge Mary Elizabeth to sell or rent the place to Silas Kemp, but best not say that here. Could give him false hopes. And could Kemp, a man of apparent modest means, buy it? Money was tight, even for a good man.

Coming to the stairs, Kemp said: "You folks go on up. I've only been upstairs twice. Once, during a rainstorm, I found a window open. It's in about the same shape, plaster down here and there."

"After all this time," Jesse said, "I think the house looks pretty good."

"It's a sweet old house," Susan said.

The boys were already racing up the stairs.

Jesse gave Susan an arm and they followed fast. On instinct, he took her to his old room at the foot of the stairs leading to the attic.

"My hang-out," he told her, crossing to his bed. To his surprise it still held his old corn-shuck mattress. He sat on it, feeling how thin it was, but decided that with a blanket or two it would do just fine.

"We'll sleep here tonight," he said.

Her eyes favored him her understanding, with a gentle amusement. "How far does it take you back?"

"About as early as I can remember. It was also my refuge. Where I could read as late as I wanted. Sleep late on Saturday. But Sunday we all went to the Cumberland Presbyterian Church in Petersburg. I moved out when I started teaching on the other side of the county at Lost Creek."

Down the hall at the next bedroom, he said: "We can put the boys in here. What do you think?"

"Yes. It's best to keep them close. And if Jamie has dreams again and wakes up crying, I want to hear him."

"We can put Gabe next door to the boys. Having an ex-slave on the same floor with the family would shock most white folks. But we're from Arizona," he said with a grin.

"Don't push him, Jesse. He may not want to. You know he's nervous about coming back to a former slave state. I really think he's afraid something might happen to him. The same state of mind about blacks must still exist for some people in Tennessee."

"I'm sure that still holds. But it's either bunk him up here or in a slave shanty, and I won't have that. I'll talk to him. Now let's go down and unload and get acquainted with what all's behind the house."

He hadn't forgotten about their guns, his Spencer carbine, and their side arms, Susan's, still that fateful Army Colt .44. Of late, guns just hadn't been uppermost on his mind. Silas Kemp, sitting on the porch, noticed, but made no comment as Jesse started by him.

"We kept these handy out in Arizona," Jesse said. "That's still Apache country. You never rode out of town unarmed, even near town. Wasn't healthy."

"I've still got my old Enfield muzzleloader and cartridge box."

"How well I remember."

"That little Spencer repeater there," Kemp said, frowning, "was a tough one. Though at Franklin, I believe, we faced more Spencer rifles than carbines."

"And from entrenchments," Jesse said, glad they

could converse a little. So far Kemp had shown no contempt for Jesse's past. Not one word, or in his manner. Which didn't mean he harbored no disdain. He was, Jesse thought, simply a somewhat taciturn man with manners.

After taking the guns and necessary bedding and clothing upstairs, Jesse showed Susan the kitchen that was enclosed in a small brick building behind the house.

"It was built separate for safety reasons," he explained. "But with both fireplaces going in the winter, you have to wonder if a kitchen in the house would have made much more of a hazard. But we were always careful. Cleaned the chimneys every year. Careful and lucky, you could say. The house never caught on fire."

The rocked well with a cedar bucket on a rope and pulley fascinated the boys, and Jesse had to draw them a bucket so they could drink from it.

"It sure is cold," Jimmy sputtered. "But good."

"Yes-sh," Jamie said. "Good."

Gabe unharnessed the mules and watered them from buckets in the wagon, then Jesse directed him to stables below the house. "There's a well there and water trough."

"Now for the smokehouse," Jesse said, gesturing onward a short way.

Made of split logs, it was longer and stood higher than the tidy kitchen. As Jesse opened the door, he released the lingering smell of hickory-smoked meat.

"Here," he told the boys, "we hung hams and bacon from that pole where we smoked them for days with logs and wood chips."

He led them on.

A neat-looking little one-door house with a peaked roof that seemed to occupy a discreet location off to one side came into view.

Jesse stopped and with a faint smile looked at Susan. "Know what that is?"

"You wouldn't try to fool me that it's not what it is, would you?"

"Wouldn't think of it, dear lady. It's a three-holer outhouse. Was always kept clean and neat, replete with mail-order catalogues for the other essential."

She frowned. "Those places always scare me. I'm afraid of snakes. Even ours in Arizona. Will you please take the boys first?"

"I will, I promise. And I'll inspect it before I do that."

Farther on, Jesse pointed to a row of four cabins and an adjacent outhouse. "Cabins . . . but actually just ramshackle shanties. My father's slaves lived there," he said flatly, more to Susan than to the scampering boys. "He freed them not long before the war. I'd like to say it was a noble gesture on his part, but it wasn't. It was a matter of cold business. By then the demand for cotton mules was falling off, and it was getting harder and harder to continue on as he had in good times. So he freed them and gave each one a few dollars and what was called free papers. That way, they could go anywhere in the South without being arrested as runaways . . . supposedly, that was it."

"Where did they go?" Susan asked.

"To cities and bigger towns."

"All of them?"

"Every last one. They wanted true freedom . . . to

go wherever they pleased. It must've been a wonderful feeling. Imagine! It was also sad. My mother wept. So did some of the older slaves. Old William was the last to leave. He was my favorite. Used to take me fishing and hunting. Showed me how to skin squirrels . . .'tain't easy, at first. I gave him what money I had at the time . . . about twenty-five dollars, I think it was. Wished him luck. We hugged and I couldn't hold back the tears and neither could he. Then he ambled off down the road out of my life. . . . While I was gone, I used to wonder if any ever came back, especially Old William. But never knew. From Old William I have learned better how to understand and appreciate Gabe. You never forget a person who was kind to you when you were growing up. Kindness to children. What a wonderful trait that is."

He had been speaking fast, from the heart. Now he said: "Guess I sort of got carried away. Here comes Gabe. I'll talk to him about where to sleep. I won't insist. And pretty soon we'd better start thinking about supper."

Susan gathered the boys and strolled back to the house.

"Been seeing into where we can all sleep tonight," Jesse greeted Gabe. "I want you to know you can take the bedroom upstairs next to the boys. That will be fine."

Gabe seemed to weigh it over and over before he said slowly: "Thank yuh, Mistuh Jesse. But Ah don' believe Ah'd feel right, sleepin' in de big house."

Jesse, not surprised by now, indicated the slave cabins. "You know what those are. But I'll be damned if I'll let you sleep there. No, sir! Wouldn't be right."

"Ah thank you ag'in, Mistuh Jesse. To tell the truth, Ah'd like to sleep in the wagon. Would be jest fine." He was growing excited. "Den Ah kin git up early an' fix breakfus' fires."

"Well, yes," Jesse agreed, relieved, thinking Susan was right. "Good idea, Gabe. You're 'way ahead of me. And before long there's a fire needed for supper."

"Yes, suh, Mistuh Jesse."

"Be a bother, carting everything in from the kitchen to the house."

"Ah knows all about dat," Gabe happily assured him. "No bother."

In the evening Jesse brought out chairs, and he and Susan sat on the front porch with Kemp while the boys played in the yard. Little was said. At last Jesse sensed a welcome ease for everyone. He could hear Gabe still rattling around in the kitchen. Over Susan's protests, Gabe had insisted on preparing the entire supper of thick cornbread, ham, gravy, baked sweet potatoes, peas, and apple pie with coffee, and, further, had waited on the table. Everyone commented on the food, Kemp more than once.

"Gabe has spoiled us all," Susan said to Kemp. "He hardly lets me in the kitchen. While we're here, I'd like to have milk for the boys. Do you know of a nearby farm?"

"There's a place on the road, up the hill a way, where you can get milk and eggs. Uriah Webb's place. You probably remember him, Jesse?"

"I do." *A fire-eater of the old school.*

As darkness moved in, the boys finally tired and came to the porch. Susan said: "Better go up to bed. Come along."

"Will . . . we hear hoot owls?" Jamie asked Jesse, with a hint of fear.

"Maybe you will. Maybe not. If you do, just go back to sleep."

"Could . . . they get me when I'm asleep?"

"Oh, no, Jamie! They don't get little boys. They don't hurt people." Jesse hugged and pulled the still-thin boy, and Jimmy put a quick arm around him, saying: "All owls do, brother, is say hoo-hoo. It's the only song they know. And when we hear that, let's say boo-boo back at 'em. Let's do that."

Susan hugged Jimmy and Jamie before starting them for the hallway where a lantern shone. She bade Kemp good night.

"I thank you folks for a mighty fine supper."

"You are most welcome, Mister Kemp. We enjoyed having you."

"Good night, Silas," Jesse said.

"You have a nice family, Jesse."

"Thank you. It's a put-together one, but we all get along. I'll have to tell you the story before long. Both boys were once Apache captives. Jamie, for some years. Jimmy, briefly. Jamie is afraid of the dark."

"Has there ever been a boy that wasn't at some time when he was little? I think I was."

After putting the boys to bed, and Jamie seeming over his scare, Jesse and Susan went to his room and sat on the blanketed bed.

"I think Jamie's fear of hoot owls goes back to when he was a captive," Jesse reflected. "I've heard that the owl is a medicine bird to Apaches. Hoots can mean good or bad."

"If Jimmy has to bring him in here, we'd better put both in bed with us."

"Now that would be a squeeze." Jesse laughed. "Well, it's been a fine day. I hope you feel better about things?"

"I do. I feel so encouraged after talking to Mister Sawyer. Right now I'm tired but happy, and hopeful."

"I'd rather have him on our side than anybody. He's practiced a lot of law and he's a fighter. Now I'm going downstairs and write that letter to Mary Elizabeth so I can get it off tomorrow. But first thing in the morning, I'll see about the milk."

Seeing that she was already beginning to nod, he gave her a quick kiss, and, sleepy-eyed, she said: "Don't be too long."

The old house seemed to creak with memories as he went down the stairs. In the shallow light of the farm office, he sat a while gathering his thoughts, feeling the presence of an austere father that had seldom laughed, who had been a come-here Southerner as a young man from Ohio. That, Jesse now thought, helped explain his total disavowal of him. Like a person taking the mantle of a new faith. His father's feelings as a new Southerner had become as devout as most and stronger than some.

And so, he began to write:

Dear Mary Elizabeth:
At last we are here!
  My family of Susan Lattimore and our two young boys, Jimmy and Jamie, and our trusted black friend, Gabe Jackson. Much has happened and the story is so

long it must wait until you arrive. After all these years, I am indeed most anxious to see you. You will like sweet Susan. She is a truly fine person. We have all been through much.

The old home place looks very good. Silas Kemp is taking excellent care of everything. Aside from the wear and tear of others moving in and out since Father died, the house looks about the same. You are more than generous to offer me the farm if I would occupy it, but my home is in Tucson. Susan and I plan to marry and return there as soon as she is freed from her husband in Philadelphia. Mr. Sawyer is handling matters for us. To say that I am looking forward to seeing you only begins to express my feelings. I am lost for more fitting words. I often think of your heartwarming letters and the many good things you sent me during the war, like underwear and knitted socks. Not to forget one particular battered box of delicious cookies that arrived as crumbs, and which I shared by the spoonful with friends while we drank Yankee coffee.

Your loving brother,
Jesse

CHAPTER FOUR

Striding up the long hill to Uriah Webb's farm, milk pail and basket in hand, Jesse had no illusions about this. But he had to face individuals as they came before him. Once he started avoiding them, actually turning tail, he would only diminish himself. Someone needed to go today, and he couldn't ask Silas Kemp to do what was his duty as head of his family.

He broke step to take in the fine two-story house painted white, the sweep of its front porch, the nodding rockers, and the massive red barn with the huge hayloft. Slave cabins beyond the barn, across from the hog pens and nearby corncribs. The long milking shed and the smokehouse twice the size of the one on the home place. Flocks of cackling chickens. The rocked well and water trough for stock. A neatly stacked woodpile. Dairy cattle grazing in the distance behind sturdy rail fences. Unseen from here, Jesse remembered, was the stone springhouse that cooled milk and butter and eggs. No pieces of broken farm equipment scattered about, the sign of a shiftless owner. Uriah Webb always kept everything in its place. Efficiency meant profits.

Jesse's father, Thomas, an efficient stockman and farmer himself, used to point with pride to their neighbor as an outstanding farmer who had been written up in national agricultural magazines. He featured Holstein dairy cattle, white Leghorn laying chickens, and raised a large number of hogs to fatten for slaughter on the corn he grew. When Uriah Webb went to town, it was said, he always had something to sell.

Jesse remembered that Webb had worked six male slaves. Worked them hard. So hard, Old William had confided to Jesse, that a young slave named Jeb had run off to Murfreesboro and Webb had tracked him down and brought him back in chains.

"Den Jeb was worked haduh den evah. An got de lash."

When Jesse asked his father about the Jeb incident, the elder said he hadn't heard of it and doubted the tale. What had happened, Jesse reasoned, was that Uriah Webb had quietly returned Jeb. It didn't look good in a Christian community to see a slave in chains, even if a slave was property. Jesse wondered if Webb had given his slaves anything when freed, and decided the answer was obvious. In one way, it mattered not: they were rich in freedom. But how had they made out? Free, yet like wanderers in a land they hardly knew beyond where they had labored.

Jesse sensed a haunting stillness and emptiness about the farm as he had at home. *Old William, where are you? I hope you haven't gone hungry.*

He walked up to the house and stood a moment before stepping up on the porch, aware of a growing reluctance. Shortly the door opened and he recognized Mrs. Eunice Webb, a round-bodied little woman of some years by now, with tired gray eyes in a kindly, wrinkled face.

"Yes?" she said, seeing the pail and basket. And upon that her gaze lifted to his face, inquiring, and then her eyes brightened with breaking recognition and she said—"You . . . you . . . are?"—and paused, putting a questioning finger to her chin.

"Jesse Wilder, ma'am," he said quickly. "Good morning, Missus Webb. I'm very glad to see you."

"Oh, yes, Jesse. . . . Yes! You've been gone so long. And you're all right?"

"I'm fine, thank you. I have my family at the home place for a short while. Waiting for Mary Elizabeth to come down from Lexington. Sure looking forward to that."

"Oh, yes! That's good."

She had always been nice, he remembered, in contrast to the gruff Uriah. The Webbs had no children. "I have two lively boys and I'd like to buy some milk and eggs, if I may?"

Her pleased expression faded all at once. "You'll have to ask Uriah. He handles all that. He's at the barn."

"Thank you, ma'am. I'm very glad to see you again."

Feeling more uncomfortable by the moment about his mission, he headed for the fenced barn. As he opened the creaky metal gate and carefully closed it before turning, a thick-set man in overalls and hat emerged from the barn. Jesse stopped.

Uriah Webb's ruddy face with a bristly ginger mustache and acquisitive eyes under bushy brows suddenly switched from the business-like greeting of a farmer expecting a buyer to surprise and instant disfavor.

"Good morning, Mister Webb," Jesse said. "I'm Jesse Wilder."

Webb didn't offer his hand, and Jesse sensed not to.

"It's been a long time," Jesse said, trying to pick up the conversation.

Webb said no word. But his eyes were busy. His compressed mouth had thinned to a slit.

"My family's at the home place for a short stay," Jesse persisted. "Waiting for Mary Elizabeth to come down from Lexington."

Webb's face was like so much stone.

"Today," Jesse said, "I'd like to buy milk and eggs, if available?"

"I have nothing for a man who was a traitor to the South," Webb replied at last, speaking with crisp deliberation. "None whatever."

Jesse had been prepared for rejection in town, a turning away rather than face-to-face insults, while keeping a tight rein on his self-control. But out in the country, in these few instants, he had been caught with his guard down. Even though he had not expected a warm renewal of what used to be between friendly neighbors, he had not expected this.

His anger was tearing loose as he said: "You do not know the true circumstances, Mister Webb, and I'm not about to explain them to you."

Webb's mouth curled. "I know enough, sir, that you served in the god-damned Union Army."

"True," Jesse stated. "West of the Mississippi. But

I never bore arms against the South, and would not have under any circumstances."

As he turned on his heel to leave, Webb shouted at him: "Traitor! Galvanized Yankee! Get off my place and never set foot here again!"

Struggling for control, Jesse yanked the gate and slammed it shut with a clang after grabbing pail and basket. Uriah Webb would never know how close he had come to getting his snarling face bashed in. And Jesse, himself now, how close he had come to self-destruction. One blow would have wrecked everything. Uriah Webb would have charged him with assault, or worse, and Jesse Wilder, who had worn the hated blue and dishonored the South and his own family, would have been found guilty at once, if he hadn't pleaded guilty, followed by prison. A blow would have complicated Susan's case by disrupting B. L. Sawyer's efforts, because Jesse would have required an attorney. And Mary Elizabeth, expecting reconciliation and peace, would have found herself in a storm of old passions.

Jesse heaved a sigh of relief. Thank God he hadn't thrown that punch.

By the time he reached the lane to the house, he had calmed down, although filled with hurt and regret. Hereafter, he knew, he must be careful how he reacted to what others said or how they acted out their accusations. But he thought: *A man can turn the other cheek only so far*.

He found Susan and the boys on the porch, the lively pair skipping back and forth.

"No milk, no eggs," Jesse gaily informed her, setting basket and pail on the porch. "Mister Webb refused to sell me anything from his land of plenty.

We had some words. Then I took my leave without a shot being fired, though I must admit that I wanted to punch him."

She stared at him with a rush of concern. "It's a good thing you didn't! Your face is still flushed. It's hard for me to believe that an old neighbor could be so mean."

"The war's not over here and won't be for a long time, Susan. It will linger even after the present unforgiving ones are gone, because there will always be the disgrace of Jesse Wilder to pass on, the Johnny Reb who wore the blue of the Union Army."

"I'm so sorry you ran into that." The boys gathered around now.

"Guess I should have expected to be turned away. Though not in so violent a manner." He shrugged. "Well, I still have that letter to mail. It's on the desk in my room. Do you happen to have a list I can fill while I'm in town?"

"I've started on one. It's by your letter. I'd take the boys and go with you, but Gabe's going to help me get some needed washing started."

"While you're working on your list, I'll harness up. My, how I miss my old saddle horse."

Gabe insisted on helping him harness the mules and hitch them to the Dougherty. Susan came out when he drove up.

"Please be careful," she said, handing up the letter and list. "I still think I should go with you." On impulse she opened a side door, stepped in, and leaned over the driver's seat and kissed him, then went out and stood beside the wagon again, waiting for him to leave.

With a teasing smile, he made the motions of a woman over a washboard and drove off.

Uriah Webb went slowly to the house, his footsteps heavy, a surging shame overriding his uncontrollable rage of moments ago. He hadn't moved until Jesse Wilder was well down the road.

Eunice was at the door, watching, and he knew that she had witnessed everything from the beginning. He brushed past her into the house without speaking.

"You didn't let Jesse Wilder get anything," she said in low voice. "Why not, Uriah? Why not?"

"And furthermore, I lost my damned temper again. Called him a traitor and galvanized Yankee. Ordered him off the farm and not to come back."

"Oh, Uriah, you had to say all that? Your temper again. Why didn't you just let him buy some milk and eggs and let it go at that?" she asked, pleading, following him.

"I wish now I could call back what I said. Thomas Wilder was a good friend and neighbor. We shared the same views on Southern rights and progressive farming. I sympathized with him when Jesse wrote that to get out of Yankee prison he had to serve in the Union Army on the Western frontier. It was that or die. . . . But Thomas couldn't see it that way. He thought the war would soon be over after Hood's defeat at Nashville and Jesse could come home. During Thomas's last illness, he struggled over whether to leave Jesse out of his will. He asked me what I thought. I wavered, but said it was his decision. So he left Jesse out."

"It's not too late to go see Jesse now and make amends."

"No. It's too late."

"Why, Uriah? Is it your pride?"

He didn't answer, but she knew that was it, and she began to weep a little and asked with half-choking sobs: "When is it ever going to end, Uriah? Pray tell me. The war took away the flower of our finest generation, and when one fine boy has to serve in the Union Army to survive the hell of a prison camp and finally come home, we turn our backs on him. . . . Yet Jesse fought for all of us . . . until wounded and taken prisoner at terrible Franklin. But in our pride we set ourselves up as high and mighty judges . . . when we should know that the Lord is the only judge of us all." She fled from him weeping.

He stood there a while longer, locked within himself, then went into the parlor after her, and presently her weeping ceased.

CHAPTER FIVE

Driving into Petersburg, Jess supposed it was Saturday by the number of people stirring in and out of the stores. Several saddle horses stood at the Southland Saloon's hitching rack. On a trade day in Tucson, in comparison, the rack would be crowded. The Dougherty was attracting eyes and Jesse noticed a few familiar faces. Nobody nodded or waved, and neither did he. *But they know me*, he said to himself, which renewed in him the cold sensation of being an outcast. By now he had grown to expect it. Once again, he lectured himself he must keep a level head.

As he had before, he parked on the first street after the square and secured the mules to a hitching post beyond a wagon and buggy.

He walked past B. L. Sawyer's office and Hanover's busy general store to the U.S. post office, bought postage from a clerk who didn't know him and actually smiled and mailed the letter to Mary Elizabeth. When could he expect her? Eight or ten days at the earliest. The train to Nashville, via

Knoxville, then by stage. Not an easy trip. Just thinking of his little sister gave him a wonderful feeling of renewal and at last closing the gap in his family.

Next, the shopping he was beginning to dread. The first item before groceries was a shirt for Gabe. He went outside and was intending to go to the general store, when someone yelled at him.

It was Marshal Burdette, striding up from down the street.

Jesse stopped. Burdette kept coming.

"I was down the street when I saw you park that freight wagon," the marshal said, puffing from his hurry.

"Freight wagon? That's no freight wagon, Marshal. It's a Dougherty passenger wagon." And Jesse thought: *Here we go again*.

"It's the size I'm goin' by," Burdette said, sounding official.

Very carefully reining himself in, blocking out his rising anger, Jesse explained: "Out West, on the frontier, the Dougherty was used either as a passenger wagon or an Army ambulance. It has side doors and step plates for easier entering."

"Reckon you know a heap about the Union Army out West, don't you, Wilder?" Burdette was stroking his mustache, a sure sign of more disagreement to come.

"Some. I've helped load men wounded in skirmishes with Cheyenne and Sioux war parties. The point I'm trying to make, Marshal, is that the Dougherty was never used to freight supplies. It was for people. This Dougherty, which I rented in Nashville, has seats like a coach. Nice for my family on the way down. Be glad to show it to you. You can step right up and be seated."

By now they had drawn onlookers.

"You can call it whatever you damned well please," Burdette snorted. "But it's the size of a freight wagon. The only time you can tie up around the square is in front of a store to pick up what you've bought."

"But, first, wouldn't you have to park it somewhere while you went in and shopped?" Jesse was starting to feel proud of himself. He hadn't yet lost his temper; instead, he had tried to reason out the problem.

A young man's snicker did it.

At that, Burdette thrust out his jaw at Jesse and ordered: "By God, you either move that freight wagon from off the square or pay a ten-dollar fine for illegal parking."

"Where do you suggest I park it?"

"The wagon yard."

"Why, that's half a mile from the square."

"Same place. The distance hasn't changed."

Holding himself in, Jesse said: "It's obvious you're determined to hound me whenever I come to town. The Dougherty is no freight wagon and you know it. That's absurd. If I take you to court, I'll prove it."

Burdette was livid. "Don't you argy with me. I'll have no galvanized Yankee disputin' my word as marshal. Now move that freight wagon!"

Jesse longed to punch him, but overcame it as self-destructive. At least he'd had his say. As he walked away, a man jeered—"Yeah, you damned Yankee."—

and it occurred to him, with local feelings against him on the rise, fueled by a blowhard marshal, he'd better start packing a handgun, but not openly. If he did, Burdette would howl that an ordinance was violated. A man had a right to defend himself.

Instead of immediately backing up and taking the street to the wagon yard as ordered, Jesse chose the back side of the square and drove around, reining the eager mules to a slow walk. Burdette was standing in front of the Southland, holding center stage, talking to a growing audience. They all turned and gave Jesse a close, hard look as he passed.

He drove to the wagon yard and found it empty. The few wagon tracks looked old. He remembered as a boy when big freight outfits used to camp here. There was a good well and freighters could buy feed. No more. Times had changed.

Walking back through a pleasant neighborhood of small, neat houses, all painted white, and, beyond, he came to a clanging blacksmith shop, a feed store, and I. P. Cole's Harness & Saddles. Cole had expanded to twice the size Jesse remembered. In a corral facing the street pranced a proud Tennessee Walking Horse. Jesse paused to admire the handsome gray. It appeared that Cole had prospered quite well. He went on, reliving what had been before the war.

French's Livery Stable appeared quieter than in the past, and the face of the barn needed painting. Slow times? Jason French, a Kentuckian, had a reputation for handling good horses. Jesse was tempted to stop and talk to him about renting a saddle horse, but not today.

Passing B. L. Sawyer's office and people waiting,

Jesse thought again how fortunate he and Susan were to have Petersburg's leading attorney.

He entered the general store and a young man came over at once to wait on him. Jesse was talking to him about the shirt when Yancey Hanover interrupted them.

"I'll see to this customer, Robert."

"Yes, Mister Hanover."

"I was about to buy a shirt," Jesse said.

"There's no law that says I have to sell you anything," Hanover said in a flat tone.

Jesse felt the impulse to wheel out of here and not take it, but forced it down. The long-buried past had to be brought up and cleared, difficult as it would be. Therefore, he let the silence settle between them.

Hanover's face was long and thin, and a drooping mustache gave him a melancholy look. His pencil-thin mouth was firm and tight, compressed in absolute denial. Mr. Yancey Hanover, sir, father of John Hanover, killed the first day at Shiloh. John and Jesse in the same infantry company. John, Jesse's best friend and a classmate at the Nashville Academy. They had enlisted together that same long-ago, carefree day, while the bands played "The Bonnie Blue Flag" and "Dixie" and the girls had smiled and waved and wept and everybody cheered. Both boys afraid the War Between the States would be over before they could shoot some Yankees. Once they got in, they had agreed, it wouldn't last long, because one Southerner could whip ten Yankees any day of the week and twice on Sunday.

Jesse could not feel anger at this expected rejection, only a sad regret and deepening hurt, with an understanding sympathy for a loving father who had lost his only son.

Jesse said: "Mister Hanover, I was hoping that someday there would be at least some faint understanding of what actually happened in a Yankee prison camp where men died like flies every day. Amid the hunger, the stink, and the guards' cruelty."

Hanover's inflexible features did not soften one particle. "I would hope," he said, "that my dear John, in the same circumstances, would never have served in the Union Army as a way out. If he had, I would not have forgiven him. I would have disinherited him as your father did you."

"Circumstances can force cruel decisions, Mister Hanover. Whether to live or die."

Hanover drew himself up. "But there's still honor and duty and pride . . . and self-respect. That's all the South has left. Now we have robed night riders in the country. People are afraid. Business is way down, there's so little money around. And carpetbaggers slinking in and a Yankee Congress bent on grinding us under its heel." His eyes flashed.

"I can understand how you feel, sir," Jesse said, speaking even more earnestly. "Now I want to tell you what I said to Uriah Webb only this morning when he refused to sell me milk and eggs for my family . . . not that they'll go hungry . . . and told me never to set foot again on his farm. He also called me a traitor and a galvanized Yankee. Marshal Burdette just called me a galvanized Yankee when he ordered me to move my passenger wagon to the wagon yard, claiming it's a freight wagon." For a briefness, Jesse feared Hanover would not hear him out, but Hanover looked straight at him, prepared to listen. "I told Mister Webb that, yes, I had served in the Union Army out West. But that I never bore arms against the South, and would not have under any circumstances. Never. I hope you'll believe me, Mister Hanover."

Turning away, Jesse walked out. Hanover did not call him back, yet neither did he shout or curse him. That was something.

After that, he needed a drink.

At the now-crowded Southland Saloon, he made his way to the bar and ordered Old Hickory bourbon. As he sipped, he gradually sensed a change in the steady hum of voices, a lessening, a shifting of feet and of faces turning his way—among them Marshal Burdette, at the end of the bar. And he realized that he had made a mistake coming in here.

But damned if he'd throw down his drink and hurry out. Between deliberate sips, he heard a low-pitched voice say: "Yeah, that's him. That's Jesse Wilder."

The bulky-shouldered man on Jesse's left, his voice sly and provoking, said: "Since when, suh, did galvanized Yankees start drinkin' good Southern whiskey?"

Jesse ignored him, as if he hadn't heard. He drew out his next sip, looking straight ahead, keeping the heckler in the corner of his gaze.

Again, louder, laced with anger: "I ast you again, suh. When did galvanized Yankees start drinkin' good Southern whiskey? Answer me. Whar's yer manners!" The speaker squared around to look straight at Jesse.

Jesse had another deliberate sip, aware that he was infuriating the drunk. It was nigh time to get out of here, but not on the run.

"Maybe he's deaf, Sam. Speak louder."

"Yeah, Sam. Louder."

Jesse took his last sip and put down the glass. When he did, the drunk raised his voice, pressing closer, and Jesse drew away and walked out of the saloon, in his wake a chorus of voices. Although feeling the burn of anger, he had to be a little proud of himself. If he had as much as pushed the heckler away, Burdette would have arrested him on the spot for disturbing the peace. There had to be a stop to this. But how? It would get meaner and the other cheek wouldn't be enough.

There was still Gabe's shirt and the groceries to get. He crossed the street to Clymer's Dry Goods, hoping that the elderly Mr. Clymer, who he hardly knew and whose first name he did not recall, would not remember him. Jesse would say nothing unless spoken to.

An obliging middle-aged clerk he didn't know waited on him and soon fetched a blue cotton shirt the right size. Jesse paid and was turning to leave with his package when he saw Clymer, coming from the rear of the store, catch sight of him and hurry to the front. As Jesse went out, he could hear a rebuking voice. Presumably the clerk was catching it. So all the store owners around the square knew that Jesse Wilder was in town today and was not to be treated cordially as a customer. Jesse was locked out, and now his hurt of knowing ran deeper than his anger.

Heading for Balmer's Groceries & Meats, he decided on a direct approach. Mrs. Doris Balmer, about his dear mother's age, had been a frequent guest at the farm with her husband Frank. She had run the grocery department with the aid of a helper, who carried orders out to wagons and buggies, while husband Frank had the busy meat department. Jesse hoped Mrs. Balmer would be there. After all these years, she, too, could have passed on and the name of the store left unchanged.

To his relief, she was up front, occupied behind the counter. There were no other customers. Entering casually, he removed his hat and said: "Hello, Missus Balmer. I am Jesse Wilder. I hope you remember me."

She looked up at him through startled gray eyes, an aproned, sweet-faced woman with spectacles and a helmet of gray hair.

"Why . . . yes, of course! I heard you were back."

"Only here for a short time, out at the farm. We're waiting for Mary Elizabeth to come down from Lexington. My wife to be, her son, and an orphaned boy."

She hurried from behind the counter to greet him, extending a plump, warm hand, which he took with a bow. "Your mother was my best friend," she said. "We grew up together."

"I remember she often spoke of you."

"I still miss her," she said, a looking back in her eyes. "We should have been sisters. We liked the same things. Shared our hopes. Confided in each other." She brightened, saying: "So you are here for a short visit, Jesse. May I ask you where you are living?"

"Out in Arizona, in Tucson."

"The desert."

"And mountains."

"And Indians."

He smiled. "Peaceful at this time."

He caught somewhat of a further sizing up in her eyes, and he ventured: "It is mighty nice to see you again, Missus Balmer. It takes me back. You are kind. I appreciate it. You see, I wasn't quite sure how you might feel after my reception on the square today."

She sent him a frown of alarm. "What in the world happened?"

Jesse recounted his experiences thus far in town.

"That is plain persecution," Doris Balmer declared, outraged, hands on hips. "I had church work to do this morning and was late, else I would have seen the whole thing. It's not unusual to hear that marshal yelling. Likes to show off. I think it's past time for the city to send Nate Burdette packing to some remote place . . . the farther from here the better." She was fed up and seemed to welcome the chance to say so. "He's an overbearing bully and blow-hard . . . lazy to boot. Hired as marshal for our town, yet spends most of his time on the square . . . in the saloon or out in front. For instance, a fifty-pound sack of sweet potatoes, dropped off for the store early one morning by a farmer, was stolen. We reported it to Burdette. He said he'd investigate. That was six weeks ago. How can he investigate from the Southland Saloon?"

Doris Balmer wasn't finished. "It irks a lot of people the way he claims he knew Robert E. Lee when Lee was a junior officer in the Mexican War. The other side of the story is that Burdette never got past the Texas border. Was a teamster. Never fired a shot in Mexico." She tucked in her lips and sighed. "My, I had my say, didn't I? Are you all right, Jesse?"

Jesse smiled, shaking his head. Then: "I don't want to make a big thing of this. Truth is I expected some turning away, some dislike, by people who didn't know the dreadful conditions in that Yankee prison and that I never served against the South, but in the Union Army in the West . . . that or die in prison. But I was surprised at the depth of their feelings . . . their total rejection. Mister Hanover refused to sell me a shirt. I didn't argue. I tried to explain what had happened in prison. He didn't change, but he did listen. At least, I got that far. I left the store with the feeling that some understanding had been reached."

She hadn't moved. Her expression remained calm, in a listening attitude. He thought he caught some understanding. Most important, she was hearing him out.

With a half smile, he said: "I still got the shirt, at Clymer's. I didn't know the clerk. Didn't say who I was. He sold me the shirt. As I went out, I saw Mister Clymer come to the front. He recognized me and I heard him getting after the clerk."

She was waiting, listening for more.

But he would leave out the near-wrangle at the saloon. He said: "After all that, I thought I might have to go out of town, even for supplies."

"No wonder," she said, and then asked at once: "What do you need, Jesse? Mister Balmer stepped out when I came in, but I can get everything, and I have a helper."

He took out the list, and they started filling it. When they had finished, he added hard candy for Susan and the boys, pipe tobacco for Gabe and himself, a dozen Florida oranges, and a sack of locally grown Jonathan apples. He paid and thanked her profusely.

"Your mother used to say that you resembled her side of the family, the South Carolina Aldens," she said, and added a hug.

That touched him. "Thank you for remembering what my mother said. My father used to tease her about the Alden men. Something he'd heard from relatives when he was courting Mother and telling her about prospects in Tennessee . . . how it was said that some Aldens spent more time in town than they did farming, chasing women and carousing, and fancying race horses that ran faster in morning workouts than they did in the afternoon."

"And what did your mother say to that?"

"She had more than one reply to save the Alden honor.

'Why, that was just Uncle Leonidas in his younger days,' she might say. 'Only one really wayward Alden in generations of statesmen and founders, and he eventually became a deacon in the church.' That would be the end of that for a while. . . . Well, I've enjoyed seeing you, and I thank you again. I'd better go bring up the wagon."

"Park out in front of the store like any customer. If you have any trouble, Burdette will hear from me in no uncertain terms. He knows I detest him."

Buoyed up with good feelings, he went out. Down the street a short way he drew back at sight of Ike Cole standing on the boardwalk in front of the Planter's House, while he picked his teeth and looked up and down the street. To avoid him, Jesse would have to cross to the other side, but that would

be too obvious and he was in a hurry now to finish a
trying day.

A long-ago scene flashed through his head as he
walked on—at the saloon on his trip back home after being mustered out of the Union Army.

*Cole, a mule and horse trader before the war, known for
sharp dealings, had recognized Jesse, and blurted out: "I
was jest about to offer yuh a drink, but damned if I will a
blue-bellied Yankee. No, siree!"*

*Something snapped inside Jesse, a breaking point, af-
ter all that had happened that day, peaked when B. L.
Sawyer had read to him the painful provisions of his father's will. And the next he knew he grabbed Cole by the
front of his vest and slammed him hard against the bar,
rattling glasses. And he was shouting into the astonished, mustached face minus its front teeth: "Shiloh . . .
Murfreesboro . . . Hoover's   Gap . . . Chickamauga . . .
Missionary Ridge . . . Atlanta . . . Franklin! Where the
hell were you?" He shook Cole's skinny frame again and
again. "You're not too old to carry a rifle. God damn you,
answer me! Did you fight for the South?"*

*The tobacco-stained mouth moved, but Cole couldn't
speak. Fear contorted the shifty face.*

*Releasing the trader like something unclean, Jesse
faced the crowd, his jaw set. No one moved. No one spoke.
They seemed somewhat embarrassed. Some had averted
their eyes.*

*He was making his way to the swinging door when a
voice broke the stiff stillness behind him. "Ike's not gonna
answer you, Jesse, because he went and got his front teeth
pulled so he couldn't bite ca'tridges an' not have to serve
in the Army. That's why."*

* * *

Thinking of the crowd in the saloon that time and the one mending voice, he thought: *There was some understanding back then.* He'd often wondered who had spoken his name.

Now Ike Cole turned and spoke to Jesse in a wheedling voice: "I heard you was back."

This Ike Cole had gold front teeth, wore a planter's hat, a gold watch chain that draped across his vest, a showy plaid suit that looked tailored, and he carried a silver-headed cane.

"For just a short time," Jesse replied, and would have gone on, but Cole faced him in such a way that Jesse would have to brush past him if he did not stop.

"Jest wondered what you might want for your farm? Country property ain't worth much now with all the trouble that's goin' on. But I can git you a fair price."

"I don't own the place. It belongs to my sister, who lives out of state, and it's not up for sale."

"Might tell her to keep me in mind." A self-importance thickened his voice. "Ike Cole. Real estate. Town and country property," he said, and handed Jesse a card. "Nobody knows the county better than Ike Cole. I've lived here all my life."

Jesse glanced at the card. He despised the man, but said: "So you've expanded?"

"Times change. Man has to change or git out. Harness and saddle business ain't what it was before the war."

Jesse left him. To his disgust, he fingered the card. He tossed it aside. He wondered where Cole got his backing for all those "fair prices" he bragged about.

Mr. Sawyer had mentioned a Lewisburg banker who was buying up property. Cole must be fronting for him. It struck Jesse as a bit out of place that a shady character like Cole could make connections with an out-of-town banker. But money made strange bedfellows.

Anxious to get along, he walked rapidly. As the wagon yard came into view, he could see only the back end of the Dougherty. In another instant, he knew that something was wrong. The wagon had been moved from where he had left it near the gate. He broke into a run and shock raced through him when he saw that the mules were missing.

Two small boys stood watching from the road.

Taut with anger, he ran up to the wagon and saw no harness on the ground as he had expected, the team just unhitched. Old habits took over. He easily tracked the shod prints back through the gate. From there he lost them on the flinty road.

He turned to the big-eyed boys. "Did you boys see someone steal my mules and lead them away?"

Both nodded.

"Which way?"

Each pointed down the road, away from downtown.

"How many men led them away?"

The older boy held up two fingers.

"How long ago did you see them do that? Was it just a little while ago?"

"Longer than that," the older one said carefully.

"You boys want to help me find my mules? I'll give you a reward."

He had two instant volunteers, and he led them down the road at a fast walk.

After a while, Jesse saw a man raking leaves in his front yard.

Jesse hastened to him. "Sir, have you seen two men leading a pair of harnessed mules by here?"

"By jingo, I did. About half an hour or so ago. I had to wonder what they were up to."

"Did you recognize the men?"

"I did not. Fairly young fellows, I'd judge. The sort you see hangin' around the saloon and pool hall."

"I'm parked at the wagon yard. They have stolen my mules."

"I'll be damned. In town in broad daylight!"

Jesse thanked him and hurried on, damning his lateness, the boys still with him.

They found the mules grazing contentedly in a pasture about half a mile on, luckily with the reins still attached. He wondered if that was by chance or if hurry had overtaken the pair.

He looked at his helpers. "How would you boys like to ride a mule back to the wagon yard while I lead? Then we'll all get in the wagon and ride to the store where we'll get your reward."

Quick nods and grins.

"But first," Jesse said, to avoid rushing them, "maybe we'd better know who we are. My name is Jesse . . . Jesse Wilder. And your name, son?" he asked, turning to the older boy.

"Richard," he said, taken aback by all this.

"And your last name?"

"Mason."

"Richard Mason. That's mighty good. And this is your brother?"

"Yes, sir. His name is Tim."

"Glad to know you, Richard and Tim," Jesse said, giving each a gentle handshake. "You've been a big help and I thank you very much. I couldn't have found my mules without you. Now, boys, as they used to say in the Johnny Reb cavalry, let's mount up!" And he boosted each one up on his own mule and told them to hold on as they swung away at a steady trot. The man raking leaves waved and the boys waved back.

"They saved the day!" Jesse called to him. "They saw the man lead the mules off, so I knew which way to go. And you helped, too, sir. Now I'm taking them to Balmer's for their reward, soon as we can hitch up."

"Yes, indeed. They deserve rewards."

Jesse hitched up fast, seated a boy on each side of him, and, as they started off, Richard asked: "Was you a real Johnny Reb?"

"Yes, I was," Jesse assured him.

"Can you give the Rebel yell?"

"You bet I can. Want to hear it?"

"Oh, yes!"

Jesse let go a piercing—*"Yee . . . haaa! Yee . . . haaa . . . haaa . . . haaa!"*—drawing it out. The mules pricked up their ears and stepped faster.

The boys sat spellbound with gaping mouths.

"Do it again!"

He yelled again to please them, this time a high, quavering screech, and then said: "That's enough, boys. But now you can say that you've heard a real Johnny Reb give the real Rebel yell."

They rolled into town at a jangling trot. He stopped in front of Balmer's, tied up, lifted the boys out, and took them by the hand into the store.

He gave Mrs. Balmer a fast account of all that had happened. "I promised these fine boys a reward.

Help us decide. I want them to have plenty."

Watching them leave after some minutes, each clutching a big bag of candy and nuts and fruit bulging from their pockets, she remarked: "They are fine little boys. I know the family. You gave them something today that's been missing in their lives. Their father, Justin, was killed at Franklin."

Jesse groaned. "How I hate to hear that." And suddenly the light had gone out of the day ending so well. "Be nice if they could go out to the farm and play with my two. They're near the same ages. Maybe that can be worked out."

"They and their mother live with her father. Circumstances are pretty close, but they make do."

Jesse kept shaking his head.

Mrs. Balmer fastened her gaze on him, her concern building. "What happened today may get worse. How will you handle it?"

"Try to keep a cool head. But I have the right to defend myself."

"Just be careful, Jesse. Use restraint."

"I understand. But a man can be pushed just so far."

She glanced away, her attention drawn to the front of the store. She said: "I see Marshal Burdette has taken position across the street now, on watch."

"Good. I want to talk to him after we load up. I'm going to complain about the mules. But I intend to hold my temper." He regarded her for a moment. "I thank you again for all you've done today, including your help with the boys."

"Just be careful. And come back."

After Mrs. Balmer's helper had loaded the groceries, Jesse walked across the street to Burdette.

"I have a complaint to lodge with you, Marshal."

Burdette puffed up at once. "What d'you mean?"

"When I went to the wagon yard for my wagon, my mules were missing. If two little boys hadn't seen two men lead them away, I'd be afoot now. I found the mules a good mile from the yard. So I'm asking you to investigate, find out who did it, and fine 'em. They'll probably brag about it at the saloon today. You'll hear 'em."

"Aw, it was just a prank, Wilder. Nothing more. Nothing to investigate." But he was starting to preen his mustache, Jesse saw, which meant he was bothered.

"It was not a prank, Marshal. It was plain old mean harassment. Furthermore, if I had happened up and caught these two in the act of leading my mules away, it would have been stealing. I would have had the right to make a citizen's arrest. To shoot, if they had resisted or attacked me."

Burdette shrugged it off, still scoffing.

Jesse spoke faster. "Another thing. When I come to town again, I intend to park my Doughtery passenger wagon by the square where passenger wagons and buggies have always been parked. If you try to run me off to the wagon yard again, I'll trot over to B.L. Sawyer's office and ask him to draw up a complaint against you for public harassment, to be filed in court."

He might as well have been telling it to the wind. Burdette stood stroking his mustache, unconcern filling his face. Jesse turned on his heel and strode to the Dougherty.

Doris Balmer flung him a cheering wave as he drove off, doffing his hat to the lady.

It was long after noon and he was wolfishly hungry. As he tore at an apple, he thought: *Mrs. Balmer is right. It may get worse. It will get rougher. But now I know what to expect. Meanwhile, avoid sure trouble, like the Southland. And it's time to keep a gun handy.*

The members of his family came out when he drove up, even Silas Kemp.

"You're late," Susan said, concerned. "We worried about you. Much longer and we'd've gone into town looking for you."

"I got delayed. A long story. But it's all right. I'll tell you about it after we unload."

"Had good news here," she said. "When I told Mister Kemp what happened this morning at the Webb farm, he went up there and came back with milk and eggs."

Jesse looked at him. "Good for you, Silas. Thank you. I felt Missus Webb would have been agreeable, if not for Uriah. That should have forewarned me what would take place in town."

After they had unloaded and gathered around on the porch, Jesse described what had happened in a matter-of-fact way. From his run-in with Burdette about moving the Dougherty to finding the mules, thanks to the little Mason boys.

Susan listened intently, in the grip of fear and anger.

"I made a mistake by going into the saloon," he said. "I won't do that again."

"You're not going to town alone again," she said.

"I doubt your being along would've made any difference when it came to the wagon."

"Oh, yes, it would have. I'd've got right in the marshal's face and told him how unfair and ridiculous he was. You've never seen me outraged."

Jesse held up his hands in mock surrender. "Hope I never do. But I don't want you fighting my fights."

"The way things are you need all the help you can get."

Silas Kemp nodded and said: "Susan's right, Jesse. If anytime she can't go with you, I will. On second thought, I believe she would've made ol' Burdette take to the tall timber."

"Thanks, Silas. But I haven't quite finished my story. He showed up again and watched while the groceries were being loaded. I went over to him and told him that, if he tried again to make me move the wagon, I'd swear out a complaint against 'im ... take him to court."

"What did he say to that?"

"Not a word. Just stroked that mustache. And I've decided this. From now on I intend to keep a gun handy when I go to town. On me or in the wagon. . . . Now, what do you say we think about supper? I'm famished."

"Mistuh Jesse," Gabe spoke up, "Ah'm on my way to de kitchen now, co'nbread on my mind."

CHAPTER SIX

Tranquil days began.

Both Jesse and Susan taught the boys. Jimmy had attended public school for a year in Philadelphia. Although Jamie had had no schooling, he was learning his letters and could write his name; proudly he would write it when asked and he was often asked. His fear, stemming from the dark past, seemed to haunt him less, and, when it did return at night, Jimmy tried to comfort him, and Jesse and Susan, hearing his cries, went to him and presently he would fall asleep.

"He can never forget what happened on the Mimbres River," Jesse said. "But time is on our side. Time and family and turning his mind toward books."

"Your old story books and texts are helpful," Susan said.

"I never could throw a book away, even when it was torn or had pages missing. I taught beginners up through the eighth grade at a little one-room country school called Lost Creek. When I applied and went before the school board, they didn't seem concerned about my credentials. They didn't ask to see the impressive diploma from the Nashville Academy I had with me. Instead, all they wanted to know was if I could keep order in the classroom. I said I was certain I could, and then was asked why. The president of the board said . . . 'Some of those eighth grade farm boys are fifteen, sixteen years old . . . stout as mules. They'll challenge you. We had three teachers quit last year . . . couldn't keep order. Couldn't whip those big boys. You still think you can handle the job?' I said yes, and the man gave me a look and wished me luck."

"Well," Susan asked, arching an eyebrow. "What happened, Mister Schoolmaster? Did the big boys challenge you?"

"Just as I'd been warned, so I really couldn't begin to teach until I'd wrestled the two biggest boys flat on their backs in the schoolyard . . . pinned 'em, in fact. Fortunately I'm a farm boy, too. Not bragging, however. It was a struggle. But I had to win or go home in disgrace."

"Jamie is such a sweet little boy," Susan said. "So affectionate. He's talking better, too. Because Jimmy is older, he looks up to him and, like brothers, I'd say, tries to match him and outdo him. Watching him grow and play, sometimes I wonder what his parents were like. Does he resemble his mother or his father? Did he have brothers or sisters? Why did they come to the New Mexico frontier? It couldn't have been an easy venture. They had to have been strong people."

"I think they were probably Texans," Jesse said

thoughtfully. "Looking for a fresh start, free from the past. Had to be farmers and small stock raisers. I spent several days on the lower Mimbres before I came to Arizona. Great climate. It's a lovely little river valley, just waiting for settlers. A young family would have everything to make a home . . . plenty of water, timber for a cabin, good grass, some land for farming, and wild game and nearby mountains. Some Mexican families had already settled up the valley when I was there."

"It sounds inviting."

"When the Southwest settles down a little more, I feel we should go back to the Mimbres and inquire around . . . ask what is known about an Apache massacre of a white family and a little boy taken away. Surely somebody would remember a name. Where they came from."

"Yes. We should do that. We owe it to Jamie. As he grows older, he'll start wondering where he came from. I hope he's not exposed to violence again. It might break him down . . . bring everything back." She sat a moment in thought. "It would be good if we could have Missus Mason and her boys out here for a week-end."

"Let's see about that. Maybe go in Friday afternoon. By that time the boys will be out of school. Drop by the store. Missus Balmer would direct me to the house."

"I'll plan on it."

Going for fireplace wood, Jesse found Gabe sweeping out a slave cabin. It bothered him, drew him across.

"Gabe, what are you doing?"

"Better Ah sleep heah."

"But. . . ."

"Wagon gits cold at night. An' Ah needs a place to keep things."

"I can see that. You need more room. But I didn't want you to feel you had to sleep in slave quarters. You can still sleep in the house."

Gabe smiled in understanding. "Thank you, Mistuh Jesse. But it don't bother me heah. Beats many places Gabe Jackson has put his head down. Nothin' colder than an ol' river bottom at night, jest covered with leaves an' branches. Afraid you'll hear bloodhounds a-bayin'. This heah is jus' fine. Come in, suh."

Jesse went in. There was a small room at the rear for the kitchen and dining and the somewhat larger front room with a fireplace, which served as a bedroom and living room. Suddenly a flood of old memories washed over him, a gentle warming.

"This was Old William's cabin," he said, strolling about. "He lived alone. His wife had died. As a boy I slept and ate here many times. Like you, he made great cornbread . . . biscuits, too, and rabbit stew. He was my special friend. Took me fishing and hunting when I got older. See that little loft? He fixed that just for me. Drove the pegs you see here into the fireplace wall so I could climb up to my bed. I thought that was great fun. Was here so much my folks would have to call me to the house."

Gabe clasped his hands and laughed. "Did you evah fall out?"

"Oh, no. I slept with my head to the back. Old William made sure of that."

As Jesse took another remembering look around, Gabe spoke, his manner a little awkward. "Thought Ah should tell you Ah been seein' a nice young woman in town."

"Be careful, Gabe, the way feelings are in town against me. I mean, if by chance some white man asked where you live, and you said here, he'd connect it right away. But I wouldn't want you to say otherwise. And if you refused to answer, which would be your right, there might be trouble."

"Ah tries to avoid all white men, yet not look like Ah am runnin'."

Jesse elbowed him gently in the ribs. "She must be good-looking for you to make that long walk to town."

"Ah don't mind. She's mighty nice. Was a slave herself on the Uriah Webb farm."

"How was she treated?"

"Good. She worked fo' de lady of de house. But sometimes she say de master used de lash on de men."

"Well, good luck, Gabe. I can see how a big handsome man from out West would catch the eyes of the local beauties."

"Mistuh Jesse, how you do talk. But Ah kinder likes it."

Friday afternoon the family dressed up and headed for Petersburg as planned. After a short distance, Jesse turned to Susan. "Have you noticed anything different inside the wagon today?"

She took a casual look around. "No. Why?"

"Look closer. Up front."

"You sound very mysterious, sir," she said, after another look. "What is it?"

"Look to my left . . . just past the seat . . . against the sideboard."

She leaned toward him and looked down. Her lips parted and she drew back in surprise. "Your handgun and holster!"

"Ready, if needed. I refuse to go unarmed after what's happened in town."

"I understand. . . . Oh, Jess, I just wish Mary Elizabeth would hurry and come, and we could hear good news from Mister Sawyer, and that we could go home and be free again."

He pressed her hand. "Shouldn't be long. Sorry I startled you. But I feel better being prepared."

"Of course, we have the right to defend ourselves," she said, slipping an arm around his waist. "It just doesn't seem right that we should have to here . . . your home, of all places."

"I know. It's changed. I doubt any of that bunch that took the mules fired a shot in the war. You don't see Silas Kemp going around with a chip on his shoulder. And he was in it to the finish. I sure never thought we'd run into this. Whatever comes, we'll see it through."

They drove on like that, close, gazing ahead, troubled, yet determined and happy within themselves. In the background of their silence, the cheerful voices of the children, the clink of harness, and the light rumble of the wagon over the rocky road.

In town, he tied up in front of Balmer's store, and escorted his family inside. Burdette wasn't in sight, but Jesse wouldn't have parked it elsewhere, the marshal be damned.

Mrs. Balmer grew excited when she saw them coming in, and, when Jesse introduced Susan as "my wife to be" and the bashful boys, everybody received quick hugs.

"Thank you for coming by," she said. "And seeing Jesse again is like seeing family," she told Susan. "Jesse's mother was my dearest friend."

"We'd like to invite Missus Mason and the boys to spend the week-end with us out at the farm," Jesse explained. "But we don't know where they live, or even Missus Mason's first name."

"Nancy . . . Nancy Mason. You'll all like her and have much to visit about. They live with her father, Mister John Sutton, a fine old gentleman and retired schoolmaster."

After she gave them an address, Susan produced a long grocery list to be filled. "I'm assuming the Masons will be free to come," she said. "If not, we'll try for later, with profuse apologies."

The modest house on Fifth Street sat well back. A rope swing dangled limply from a tired-looking oak tree, the center of attention in the beaten yard.

Before Jesse could step down to tether to the ring in the iron hitching post, Susan hesitated, saying: "Maybe you should go first? See if it's all right?"

Going to the front door, he could hear the voices of a woman and the young boys. He rapped lightly and the voices ceased. Then light footsteps and the door opened. A slim, brown-haired woman with a heart-shaped face and wide brown eyes regarded him.

He'd already removed his hat. "Ma'am, I'm Jesse Wilder. Missus Mason?"

"Jesse Wilder? Oh, my goodness. Boys, come here!"

"My family is with me," Jesse hurried. "We've come to invite you-all to spend the weekend with us."

"Please bring them in, Mister Wilder."

He waved, and Susan stepped down, taking each boy firmly by the hand.

Once Jesse made the introductions at the door as he had at the store, Susan said: "We apologize for descending on you like this, Missus Mason."

"It's Nancy. You are most welcome. And here are my boys. Richard and Tim. Please come in."

The boys sized each other up with outright interest as they all went in. When seated in the modest parlor, Nancy Mason exclaimed: "I'm so glad you've come! All I've been hearing is about you, Mister Wilder, and the mules, and the boys' ride on the mules and in the wagon, and the more than generous rewards you gave them at the store. All told and retold in great detail."

"And the Rebel yell," Richard insisted.

She shushed him with a quick, pointed finger. *We don't talk about the war.*

Jesse said: "If it hadn't been for Richard and Tim, I'd never have found the mules. I won't say they were actually stolen. But they were led some distance from the old wagon yard and left so I wouldn't find them. Richard and Tim saw them taken down the road, and they told the truth as boys should. Ever since, Susan and I have been hoping you and the boys could come out."

"Yes, indeed," Susan said. "We hope you can today. And we can wait, with profuse apologies, for you to get ready."

"I don't know," Nancy Mason said uncertainly. "Father isn't here. But he should be back soon."

"Is it all right if we wait until he returns?"

"Oh, yes."

After a pause, while all the lads fidgeted, Nancy Mason suggested to Richard: "Why don't you and Tim show your visitors the swing? But be careful."

"We will be."

Jesse nodded, and the four of them dashed out.

This was the time, he sensed uncomfortably, to express their feelings to Nancy over the death of her husband Justin at Franklin, painful as it would be for her in bringing up the past. But it should be done.

"Missus Mason," he said, "Susan and I want you to know that you have our heartfelt sympathy over your loss of Justin."

"Oh, yes," Susan said.

Nancy Mason looked at them through tired eyes. "Thank you so much. You are most kind. It's still hard for the boys to grasp why it happened and why there was a war, fighting Yankees. They often ask about their father. Richard, who was born in July of 'Sixty-Two, thinks he remembers his father, but it's wishful thinking . . . Franklin happening the last day of November of 'Sixty-Four. Tim was born early in 'Sixty-Four. I tell them what he was like and show them his tintype. . . . It's difficult for me."

"We understand," Jesse said. "I was wounded at Franklin. I woke up in a Yankee hospital . . . from there to a Yankee prison camp. You may have heard the rest of my story?"

She was puzzled. "No. . . ."

"I won't go into it now. Not important. We just

want to extend our sympathy to you and the boys. So you'll know that we care. And I think I should tell you that Susan lost her husband James at First Manassas in Virginia . . . Union Army."

Susan's expression of reproach told him that would have been better left untold. *This moment is for Nancy, not me.*

Now the women regarded each other, their eyes softly locked. Tears glistened. Suddenly they rose and embraced. After a moment they parted, and Nancy, dabbing with a handkerchief, murmured: "I need this. I haven't had a good weep in a long time. Thank you-all for coming." She looked at Jesse. "Thank you for telling me you were at Franklin. Now I can share something of what happened on that terrible day."

Moved, he stood and put his arm gently around her, patted the back of her head, and stepped back.

"Now," she said, smiling, "we can get down to visiting. I've been an awful hostess. But first I'd better take a peek at what's going on at the swing."

"I will," Jesse said, going to the doorway and looking out. "Your Richard is swinging our Jamie."

"Good. They're getting along. I've tried to teach the boys to share with others. I tell them that to have friends, they have to be friends. But that they must not let others run over them, and that they must look out for each other. I wish there were more boys near their ages in our neighborhood."

"Our boys need playmates, too," Susan said. "If your visit can take place, I know all four will have a fine time. And we'll fix up a lot of good things to eat."

Nancy Mason was looking more relaxed and content by the moment. "While we wait," she said, "I think it would be proper if I serve you some of my father's wild grape wine. Think you would like that?"

"Of course," Jesse and Susan said in unison.

Nancy went into the kitchen and appeared back shortly with glasses of dark red wine on a small silver tray. She served them graciously, went back, and returned with a glass for herself.

Jesse raised his glass. "Here's to you, Nancy, and all your family."

"You-all are indeed kind and thoughtful. And my sincere best wishes to all of you."

After they had sipped in silence for several minutes, Nancy said: "It is a bit nippy. Father is careful not to serve it to everybody, especially church members. He would never admit it, but I think he is rather proud of his wine-making."

"It's just the way I like it," Jesse said, smiling. "It has authority."

They chatted on, with Susan informing Nancy: "We don't plan to stay very long at the farm. Our home is in Arizona. Jesse's sister Mary Elizabeth Somerville is coming down from Lexington to see us."

"The place is hers," Jesse said. "The only reason we've come back is to bring the family together again. Been a long time."

"I remember Mary Elizabeth," Nancy recalled. "She was always friendly . . . very pretty. She is some years younger than I. I don't remember seeing her after Justin and I married and lived in Shelbyville."

"I didn't know Justin," Jesse said, speaking carefully, hoping he wasn't stirring old embers too much. "May I ask how you two met?"

She responded at once, with apparent gladness. "I met him at a country dance. Another girl and I had slipped off with her brother. The fiddle music was lively . . . made us want to dance. It was very exciting to both of us, never having been to a country shindig. There was some drinking. You could smell the whiskey when you talked to a boy. My friend said . . . 'There's that tall, good-looking, blond boy from Shelbyville. They say he's a very good dancer.' I said I thought he acted stuck-up and wasn't cute at all."

Nancy Mason talked without restraint now. A hidden liveliness sparkled in her eyes and face and her voice was sweet with remembering.

"Well," she continued, "I danced with several boys. Then Justin asked me. To my surprise, I found that he wasn't stuck-up as I'd thought. He just stood very straight and composed. Instead, he was friendly and nice, and said funny things and seemed to get better-looking as the evening went on." She kept smiling. "He asked where I lived, and I told him and asked where he lived. . . . We started writing each other. Then he came over to see me. He was working in his father's hardware store in Shelbyville. He'd ride over on Sundays." She paused and looked at them with apology. "Sorry to go on like this, but I haven't talked to anyone about Justin in a long time."

"It's good for you and we are glad to know how you met," Susan encouraged. "It's a sweet story. Why, I virtually tracked Jesse down out in Arizona because I needed his help. When did you and Justin marry?"

"Not long after the war started. There was so much uncertainty. He volunteered a few months later, as so many did in 'Sixty-One, but managed to come home a few times. That way he left me the boys." She brushed away a tear.

An elder's voice mingled outside with that of the boys', and presently an arresting man, tall and straight, with blue intelligent eyes and iron-gray hair and a full beard entered the room. John Sutton showed a schoolmaster's reserved mien until Nancy made the introductions, whereupon he bowed, smiling at Susan and shaking hands with Jesse, a most courteous gentleman of the Old South.

"Father, they've invited us to spend the weekend at the Wilder farm," Nancy said, leaving it hanging for his approval.

"I think it would be good for the boys to get out in the country for a change. You as well. . . . Mighty nice of you folks."

"We'd love to have them," Susan said. "We've been thinking about it, and on the spur of the moment decided to come in today. We realize it rushes Nancy."

Nancy swept them all a look. "Then we'll go." She called her boys from the doorway, and they came on the run. Jimmy and Jamie were trailing, faces flushed.

While the Masons hurried about packing, Sutton said to Jesse: "I knew your father rather well. He was strong for education and deplored the lack of funds and facilities. We used to talk about what it would take to establish a small liberal arts college here." A subtle amusement spread across his face. "With John Sutton as president. But it wasn't possible then and still isn't. I mean the college. . . . Let's see, I believe he sent you off to the Nashville Academy, where you were an honor student."

Jesse nodded, pleased that Sutton would remember.

"And then you taught at . . ."—frowning, searching for the elusive words—"at Lost Creek."

"You have a good memory, sir."

"How did it go?" Behind the question was a certain perceptive inquiry.

"There had to be order before there could be school. That came after I'd outwrestled the two biggest boys. They'd run off several teachers. The school board had warned me."

Sutton raised his right hand. "Exactly. You had to have order first. About the same experience I underwent at my first school, a little one-roomer 'way east of here called Hickory Ridge. A family had moved into the district from Kentucky. On the first day of school the well-meaning father brought in his two big, hulking sons, Homer and Jed. He took me aside. 'Mister Schoolmaster, if you can teach my boys to read and write, I'll be eternally grateful to you,' he said. I assured him I would do my best, sounding like young George Washington. He took me by the arm, saying . . . 'It won't be easy. They're headstrong. Like young bulls. Take after the other side of the family. If you have any trouble, let me know. And, when they come home, they'll git a lickin' from me they'll never forget."

Sutton pulled on his beard and resumed in a recalling tone: "I had a short session opening day and nothing happened. But on the second day they started talking out loud and mimicking bird sounds. I told them to stop . . . they didn't. I had to take action then or there would be no school. I said . . . 'You two boys step outside. Rest of you kids stay seated.' I could see the little girls were getting scared, and that bothered me."

"Did Homer and Jed refuse to go out? Why, no. That was what they wanted. They'd whupped other teachers, run 'em off. I told them . . . 'Either behave or go home and take a licking . . . those are your father's words.'

"Homer said . . . 'We ain't goin' home. We'll stay and do as we please. We don't fear you.' I said . . . 'Then take your licking here.' It was pure bravado on my part. I was hoping I could talk some sense into them. But to no avail. I could see their idea was to wrestle me . . . that was their long suit. They were muscled up like Turkish strongmen, Homer especially. I had to keep him off me. Then he came at me, his stocky arms set to grapple. Fortunately I have long arms. I bloodied his nose and danced away. He lunged at me, mad and surprised. Jed yelled . . . 'Git a-holt of 'im, Homer.' When Homer rushed me again, I dodged and hit him in the eye. He yelled and tried to bear hug me. I dodged and hit him on the jaw, and he stumbled and fell. A lucky punch. I was desperate. You see, Homer was powerful but slow. Jed yelled . . . 'Git up, Homer. Whup that teacher. What'll the kinfolks back in Kaintuck say when they hear a skinny book-reader licked you?'"

Sutton held back, as if he might be boring.

"Go on, Mister Sutton," Jesse urged. "Finish the story. I can understand how it was."

"Well, Homer jumped up and charged me like a mad bull, his hands groping. He grabbed my arm. I tore loose. He came on, hands high. That left his middle open. I couldn't dodge him this time, he was so close, so I had to hit him. I did, in the stomach, with all my desperate, skinny strength. When he gave a big gasp and doubled over, I hit him on the jaw and he fell flat on his back, looking up at me in a puzzled way. I waited for Jed to rush me, but he just stood there, looking down at Homer with his mouth open. I had to act now when I was on top. I said . . . 'Come on, Jed. You're next.' When he didn't come at me, I said . . . 'You boys have two choices. Go back in that schoolhouse and behave yourselves, or go home and take the damnedest licking you'll ever get.'"

A withholding pause.

"What happened then, Mister Sutton?" Jesse asked.

"We had school."

Jesse and Susan laughed and applauded.

Nancy came in with the boys, carrying a light handbag. "I gather that my dad was telling you how he became a country schoolteacher."

"Quite a story," Jesse said, "and I learned that we both had similar experiences, if there was going to be any book learnin'. On the first day of school it was muscle over brain matter."

"And a lucky punch or two," Sutton admitted.

"Your father is a very modest man," Jesse insisted. "It is a privilege to know him. . . . And, sir, we'll have your family back Sunday afternoon."

"It was a pleasure to see you and Susan and the boys."

They left in a rising chatter of young voices, and, as they drove by the store, Mrs. Balmer came out and waved. Everybody waved back. Marshal Burdette, in front of the saloon, touched the brim of his hat and nodded, and Jesse nodded back.

Looking back at the enjoyable visit, Jesse thought: *No stiffness in greeting. No holding back. Nancy said she didn't know, but Mr. Sutton must be familiar with my past. He was just too much of a gentleman to say anything.*

Jesse couldn't have appreciated it more.

CHAPTER SEVEN

Jesse let the mules plod along for the enjoyment of his passengers. Susan and Nancy were starved for woman talk, and, judging from what he could tell, the boys were at ease with each other by this time. There would be plenty left to visit about later and to clarify relationships. Nancy had introduced them to her father as family, and in the rush Jesse had explained no further.

When they pulled up at the house, Gabe was waiting, and, as he unhitched and led the mules off, Nancy commented: "How nice. Like old antebellum days. Though not at our house. Just a dear old woman who helped my mother for years and left like the others when freed."

"Gabe Jackson joined our family under most unusual circumstances out in Arizona," Susan said. "A story worth telling later."

Jesse and Susan took their guests upstairs to the extra bedroom, made up that morning. Coming down the stairs, all the boys started jumping from step to step with resounding effect until that got out of hand and was stopped.

At Nancy's request, Jesse showed her around the house.

"I like all the space," she said. "The gracious parlor and the grand stone fireplace."

Then they strolled out on the porch and visited while the lively young ones played in the yard, scarcely a pause as they ran and jumped.

As they watched, Susan remarked that she and Jesse were teaching Jimmy and Jamie to help make up for lost schooling time. "Jamie was an Apache captive for several years until Jesse and others rescued him."

"Apache captive!" Nancy cried.

"Jimmy, too, for a very short time. That's how I came to know Jesse out in Arizona. Another story to tell you. Jamie is learning his letters and loves to write his name . . . is proud to. At least we think Jamie is his given name, as best as we could make out, and as he responded to it. His parents were murdered right before his eyes in New Mexico. He still carries that horror in his mind, cries out at night sometimes, and we're trying hard to push it further and further back in his memory. Not that he could ever forget it."

"How horrible for a little child."

"Schooling will help."

"And love."

"Oh, yes, and Jimmy helps a lot. He's taken on the rôle of an older brother. They do fuss now and then though, being boys."

"Actual brothers do as well. As for schooling, my father, the schoolmaster, thinks it's time for me to go

back to school ... where and how he can't say ...
and work toward becoming a full-fledged teacher.
Better than clerking now and then in stores. He has
the influence to get me started as a substitute."

"You'd make a fine teacher," Susan said. "You
have much patience."

"It is heavy on my mind. But I'd have to leave Fa-
ther, say Nashville or elsewhere, for higher educa-
tion courses to go with my high school diploma.
And I don't think I should leave him alone, since
Mother's gone. Too, he's a godsend with the boys.
I'd hate to leave him."

"I can well understand your feelings," Jesse said.
"Be nice if you could take some summer school
courses not too far from home." He shook his head.
"I'm no help. I've lost touch with everything back
here."

"Nevertheless, I appreciate your thoughts. I need
to talk to somebody."

"This does occur to me," he said slowly. "Maybe
there are courses you could take by mail? Maybe
from the state university? That should impress the
local school board. Write and ask. Don't give up.
Your father must know of other schools to write to."

"I hadn't thought of that. Neither has Father. He's
getting on in years. His thinking is in the past. We're
both like the farmer who has a field he knows needs
plowing for planting. Only he doesn't have a mule
to pull the plow ... not even the plow."

Jesse and Susan both laughed.

As suppertime approached, it was time for much
washing of grimy young hands. When they entered
the dining room, Jesse introduced Silas Kemp without reference to Franklin.

Gabe, who had baked bread and made apple pies, took over the serving from Susan, who explained: "Gabe feels that the dining room, like the kitchen, is his domain. He's a marvelous cook. He says he can cook anything that's fit to eat, including game. He had to learn that in order to survive as a runaway. Among his favorites are Mississippi River catfish and turtle soup and squirrel dumplings. I could go on."

"Uncle Gabe makes good cornbread, too," Jimmy vouched.

"We're trying to bring the boys up to appreciate the finer things in life," Jesse said with a grin.

As Gabe entered from the kitchen with another dish of steaming vegetables, Jesse said: "We're bragging on you, Gabe."

"Don't spoil de cook, Mistuh Jesse. Might make 'im lazy an' no-account."

"This is a fine dinner," Nancy complimented.

Silas Kemp seconded and, turning to Nancy, said: "I'm here to look after the place for Missus Somerville. Jesse and Susan have very generously invited me to sit at their table."

"And Silas sees that we get plenty of milk and eggs from the Uriah Webb farm," Susan said.

Kemp shrugged it off.

By early evening their active day had caught up with the boys, and, after they had been put to bed, Jesse suggested adjourning to the parlor.

"I remember coming here with my father when I was a kid," Nancy told Jesse. "While the men talked, your mother would take me out to the flower garden. And I'd go home with a bouquet."

In this restful pause, the thought pressed Jesse

that some explanation was due after what had been mentioned about Gabe at supper. So he said to Nancy: "We should tell you more about Gabe Jackson. How he came to our family. He's a very interesting man, strong and good. The boys love him. He was a runaway from an Alabama plantation. Lived in the woods for some time. Cut wood for steamboats on the Mississippi. In New Orleans he cared for a sweet ol' preacher man, as he called him, who taught him to read the Bible. Yes, Gabe can read. How about that! His old friend passed on, and Gabe headed west. Joined our rescue volunteers. Now I'd better have Susan tell you how all this came about."

Little by little, beginning with Jimmy's capture, Susan began to relate what had happened, briefly and concisely. Jesse broke in now and then to supply details which he thought important or when she skipped a crucial part, including how the Army deserters were put down.

"It would sound like bragging," she would protest.

"It's an essential part of the story," he would insist. "You surprised the ringleader and shot him. He didn't expect a woman to have a gun. That gave the rest of us time to get the others."

"It's a wonderful story," Nancy said, awed. "Like a fairy tale. How you, Susan, managed to find Jesse. How did you even know where to begin to search for him?"

"My search began after reading about Jesse in newspapers," Susan began, and proceeded to tell the story. "Finding him," she finished up, ". . . it was almost as if something had led me to him in Tucson."

A kind of reverence seemed to hold them all until Jesse broke the silence. "And that a homeless little boy . . . his mind filled with horror . . . should come to us by chance . . . to brighten our lives and give Jimmy a little brother, and we to give him a home without fear."

Susan looked at him. "That was well said. Now please tell Nancy about Rutherford."

"I know it's easier for me than for you," Jesse said, as he explained the situation from the beginning to the present. "Mister Sawyer is representing us," he said in conclusion. "There is no better man. We'll probably have to go to Philadelphia."

"I hope it works out for you-all," Nancy said. "You've been through so much."

"There is still one story left," Jesse said. "It's mine," which he then set forth with a terse account of conditions in the prison camp. "As I told Mister Hanover at the store, I volunteered to wear the Union blue out West to save my life from that terrible place. Your father must know how I'm regarded as an outcast and traitor. How my own father disowned me. But Mister Sutton was too much of a gentleman and too understanding to bring it up to me."

"I, too, understand," Nancy said, near tears. "May God bless you and Susan and your boys and make everything right again for you."

In the morning, while rummaging through his closet, Jesse found a sack of marbles from his schoolboy days. With a surge of pleasure, he knew he'd found just the game to keep the young ones interested for a good while.

"We're going to play marbles," he informed them in the front yard, and held up a colorful agate for them to view. "This is a taw, which you use to shoot at other marbles on the ground." To demonstrate, he kneeled and put the taw between his right thumb and forefinger and shot it, while his audience watched agape. Then he picked out a pretty taw for each boy, and they all got down on the ground and began practicing, Jesse showing them just how to hold their shooter. To make it a game, he drew a circle and placed several marbles in the center and told them to start shooting.

After a short while, Richard knocked a marble out of the circle and yelled: "Got one!"

Seeing that Jamie and Tim had difficulty holding their taws just right, Jesse showed them how to close their fingers and thumbs and nestle the taw for the shot, with the back of the hand flat. The older boys learned faster, so to avoid likely brotherly clashes Jesse left the first circle for them and drew another for Jamie and little Tim and placed marbles therein. They all settled down to some serious playing, while Jesse stood by assisting. With that going well, he remembered another game and drew a line and instructed them to toss their taws and see who could come nearest the line. They also liked that.

Before they returned to their passion for shooting, he distributed the remaining marbles in the sack to them to keep. "Put these in your pocket," he said. "You might try all your marbles now for taws. Maybe you want a heavier one or a lighter one for the best shooter."

At this juncture Nancy Mason, who was sitting

nearby, said: "Boys, have you forgotten what you say when somebody gives you something nice?"

"Thank you! Thank you!" they shouted, emphasizing the words with much jumping up and down. The Wilder kids joined in as well. And then they all returned to trying out the taws.

"Where did you ever find the marbles?" Susan asked.

"I was looking in my closet for an old book."

"Well, it was quite a discovery."

"I won't tell them about a game we used to play called keepers."

"It sounds like possible trouble."

"It was then and still is. You put so many of your marbles in a circle and the other boy takes an agreed number of shots. He gets to keep what he knocks out of the circle. Then it's your turn. A crack shot can clean up. There was an older boy in town we country boys learned not to play against. He always took us, using a heavy taw."

"What about playing friends?"

"You played more for fun. You won a few. You lost a few. Maybe you'd put just one marble in the circle. And sometimes we'd trade marbles."

That afternoon the boys were back at marbles when Gabe appeared with what at a glance looked like a bundle of long sticks. He marched boldly in, smiling in a secretive way.

Susan started to speak, but didn't want to spoil his surprise.

Her boys took one quick look and, rushing to him, yelled with delight: "Stick horses! Uncle Gabe's got stick horses!"

"Indeed, Ah do. One fo' each good boy."

He sat the bundle down on end and, for show, held up a narrow piece of wood, straight and smooth, about four feet long. A short strand of rope wrapped around one end served as a bridle. Motioning Jimmy and Jamie to wait, he handed stick horses to the other two. When all had a horse and Gabe saw the Masons just held theirs, not mounting, he said to Jimmy and Jamie: "Now, ride. Show your friends how to ride a wild stick hoss."

They took off, yelling. Richard and Tim mounted fast and rode after them with yells.

"Richard and Tim have never had stick horses," their mother said. "What a nice thing to do."

"Gabe made stick horses for the boys in Arizona," Susan said. "He's always thinking up ways to entertain them."

After breakfast on Sunday, Gabe told Jesse and Susan he was going to take a friend to church in town, and assured them there was plenty of everything on hand in the kitchen.

"What he means is," Jesse said, winking at Susan, "he'll be taking a pretty woman to church."

"I can't think of a better reason," she said.

"We'll be going in this afternoon to take home Missus Mason and the boys," Jesse said.

After a lazy morning and a late lunch and a leisurely ride, it was into the afternoon when they reached the house. John Sutton came to the door and out on the porch as they drove up. Richard and Tim could hardly wait to run up to him. "Look, Grandpa! Look at our stick horses!"

"Well, can you ride 'em?"

"Just look!" And they mounted their steeds and raced into the yard.

"We've had a most wonderful time," Nancy told her father. "Jesse and Susan spoiled us. Everything was so enjoyable. Their cook is a former slave they met out in Arizona . . . made the stick horses, too. The boys played to their hearts' content every day. And had marble games and ran foot races. They went to bed early and we caught up on some visiting."

"Just what you and the boys needed. It's good to get out in the country for a change. Now, you folks, please sit down. I refuse to let you get away so soon. You see, Jesse, there's a fitting sequel to the story I told you the other day about Homer and Jed which I have to tell you."

"I'd like to hear it," Jesse said readily.

When everyone was seated, Sutton said: "A number of years later long after I had left Hickory Ridge, moving up the teaching ladder, one little rung at a time, a husky-looking man came by here to see me. He knocked politely and said . . . 'My name is Homer Hays, Mister Sutton. I doubt that you remember me, but I sure remember you.' I had to laugh and said . . . 'Oh, yes,' and invited him in. He could hardly wait to say . . . 'That was the best thing that ever happened to me. You did me a huge favor. It straightened me out.' I asked him what he was doing. And he said that after he and Jed had finished the eighth grade at Hickory Ridge, the family had returned to Kentucky, and Homer had taken more schooling around Lexington. 'Now would you believe it, Mister Sutton, I'm a schoolteacher . . . the eighth grade!' I warmly congratulated him and asked if he'd had any trouble with the big boys.

" 'Only on the first day.' I had to chuckle. And brother Jed? Well, Homer said Jed wasn't much of a fighter and had taken up backwoods preaching. He'd always liked to tell other people what to do. I then told Homer that the day after he and Jed graduated from the eighth grade, their proud father came to see me. He gave me the best tasting smoked ham I've ever had and a jug of smooth bourbon meant to be sipped, not drunk."

John Sutton had other stories to tell about teaching in the early days, while the young played without let-up in the yard, on the swing or racing fleet stick horses.

It was the middle of the afternoon when Jesse and Susan said good-bye. Would they see each other again? That palpable unknown rose before them with its regret, but vanished quickly amid smiles and hugs and handshakes. Nancy and her father went out with them, and, at her prompting, Richard and Tim voiced their thanks and waved as Jimmy and Jamie waved from the departing wagon.

"Maybe Nancy will meet some nice young man who likes boys," Susan said hopefully when they were out of earshot of the house.

"Could be. But from what I've seen around town, the field is pretty lean of eligibles. I hope the school teaching works out, slow as it is. She'll meet nice people."

Susan gave him a keen look. "You sound very down on your home town."

"Probably unfair, but it's based on what I've seen in the saloon and the bunch that follows Burdette around. Yes, Petersburg is better than that."

They left the square and entered the outskirts of

town when Jesse heard shouts and cries in the distance. Farther on, where the road skirted a scattering of oak trees, he saw a surging crowd of twenty or thirty men. Some held horses.

"What are they doing?" Susan asked nervously.

"They're up to something," he said, slowing the mules. "I don't like the looks of it."

The voices reached a higher, ominous peak, like a pack in full cry. Jesse spotted a crush of struggling bodies. He saw a man toss a rope over the lowest limb of an oak. And another, standing in the stirrups of a saddler, knotted the rope and made it secure. The tugging and wrestling and punching never ceased.

Jesse caught a flash of fighting black flesh, and suddenly a sick feeling gripped him. The black man was putting up a mighty struggle for his life as fists flew. In the next moment there seemed a lull in the action, yet the yelling rose higher and higher. Then Jesse saw the black man, naked to the waist, being hoisted to the back of a bay saddle horse, hands tied behind him.

Shock tore through Jesse. "My God ... that's Gabe they're going to hang!" Susan screamed. Jesse was lashing the mules even as he shouted, and they took off in a startled run. In his haste the short distance seemed far. The saddle horse, spooked by the crowd, kept dancing about despite yanking by its holder while the hangman fashioned a loop and moved toward Gabe.

There was still time.

Knowing the mules must be stopped or there'd be a runaway, Jesse yanked on the heavy iron brake lever and felt the rub blocks push hard against the rear wheels. The mules slowed. Jesse kept yanking with one hand and pulling mightily on the reins with the other. As they drew up to the scene, now a shouting, cursing mob, the mules slowed to a tugging halt and Jesse locked the brake in the racket frame. The team couldn't run now.

The fractious horse was still delaying the hanging. A man ran up to assist the holder and seized the bridle, and together they brought the bay around on the bit toward the hangman.

Jesse grabbed his handgun from the holster against the sideboard and leaped out, running, shouting: "Stop it! Stop it!"

Startled faces turned on him accusingly. "Get back! Stay the hell back there!"

Jesse shouldered past several men, his eyes fixed on Gabe, hunched down in the saddle, almost stoical.

Whiskey fumes rode the air. A man half lunged at him, staggering. Jesse shoved him aside with his left arm.

The man snarled: "I say git back! Who th' hell are yuh?"

"It's Jesse Wilder!" a relishing voice shouted back. "Jesse Wilder . . . the galvanized Yankee! Traitor to the South!"

Jesse kept going toward Gabe, shouting: "Stop it! Stop it!"

"Stand clear, Wilder!"

"Hurry up! Hang that uppity nigger!"

Now, before him, with the horse near being under control, the hangman stood poised to loop the noose over Gabe's head, ever mindful of the hooting approval urging him on.

The hangman was Ike Cole. Gold teeth shining. Planter's hat at a rakish angle.

Jesse waved his six-shooter at him, shouting: "Stop it, Cole! That man works for me! He's a free-man! His name is Gabe Jackson. Now step back and stop this!" *If he could just calm this down long enough to get Gabe down off that horse.*

As if he must put on a show of propriety for all, Cole puffed up and yelled back: "This here nigger got uppity with me this mawnin' in town! Wouldn't git off the sidewalk. Wouldn't tip his hat to me."

"Nobody has to tip his hat to you, Ike Cole. You had your front teeth pulled so you couldn't bite cartridges . . . that way you got out of serving in the war. Everybody knows that, Ike."

"Like hell!" Cole denied through his surprise.

"So let him go!" Jesse demanded.

Instead, Cole turned to Gabe with the noose.

At the same instant Jesse saw that, if the two men released the horse just as Cole got the noose on, Gabe would hang.

"For the last time, stop this or I'll fire!" Jesse yelled at Cole.

Cole ignored him, almost taunting, tense, ready, waiting, standing on the balls of his feet. The lead horse, still fighting the bit, was forced closer. Gabe dodged quickly as Cole made a tentative try with the noose.

Jesse was going to shoot Cole when a slurred voice snarled in his ear: "You ain't gonna shoot no-body, Yankee!"

Jesse felt a swinging blow across his left shoulder that knocked him off balance, nearly to the ground.

Simultaneously he heard the blast of a gun and, twisting around, saw Cole's hat fly off. And Cole, jerking, dropped the noose like a hot iron, his gold-toothed mouth wide in astonishment as he hunkered down in fear.

Jesse stared at the wagon. There stood Susan, gripping a smoking Colt, while the hang-rope crowd stood thunderstruck.

"Stop it!" she cried shrilly. "Let him go!"

Now is the time, Jesse thought. He moved, grabbing Gabe down from the saddle of the plunging horse. The frenzy of the moment was broken. They wouldn't dare shoot a woman. He took Gabe swiftly through the stunned watchers. No man tried to stop him. No man cursed him. Some even stood back.

"I didn't favor this from the start," he heard one say in a tone of relief. "Just came along to watch." Another muttered: "Ike Cole stirred up the whole thing."

"Too much whiskey," another put in.

There was Marshal Burdette, with the air of an interested spectator.

Jesse drove his voice at him. "Marshal, why didn't you stop this?"

"It's outside the city limits."

"Shame, Marshal! Shame. You condoned murder. Would it have made any difference inside the city?"

As Burdette turned his back and walked away, Jesse thought: *The son-of-a-bitch. Did he know that Gabe's with me? Was that part of it?*

The children were crying as Jesse hurried Gabe up and inside the wagon and freed his hands. Susan was shaking, but she still gripped the Colt as she continued to watch the quietly dispersing crowd.

"You did it again," Jesse marveled, grasping her

shoulder. "Just like with the deserters. My God, you are brave, Susan. I didn't even know you had the gun with you."

"It was in my purse."

"Like before," he said. "Let's go home."

He released the brake, laid on the leather, and they rushed away. When he looked back, Gabe was holding both boys. Big tears rolled down his battered face. His voice came out soft and tortured: "Mistuh Jesse an' Miz Susan. M'brave, sweet friends. You saved m'life. Ah thanks you. God bless you. . . . De sweet ol' preacher man's words in New Awlins come back to me now. He said if you believe in the Lord, good things will happen to you someday. Thank you, Mistuh Jesse, Miz Susan."

Seeing Gabe's swollen face and upper body, Jesse said: "For the first time in my life, I'm ashamed of my people here. Just how did it start, Gabe?"

" 'Bout like de hangman said. Ah was walkin' down de street on my way home after church. Ah sees him come out de back of de saloon, which Ah reckon stays open on Sunday, though de Lord's day. He looked at me, says . . . 'You forget to tip your hat, nigger!' Ah didn't say a word . . . kept right on walkin'. Den he say . . . 'Git off de walk, nigger. Git in de street where you belong.' Ah didn't. Kept walkin' fast." Gabe swallowed hard. His voice broke. "Ah heard shouts. Soon Ah heard men comin' on foot. Dat hangman in de lead. One man on horseback. Dey took me to a barn . . . beat me up. Dey ran outta whiskey, went back fo' mo'. Held me till de hangman say go."

Jesse just shook his head. "We're lucky Susan is such a great shot." He took her hand, while he let the mules ramble. "Shooting Cole's hat off, instead of him, was the best possible way to stop it. I was prepared to shoot him when I got knocked out of the way. But if I'd shot Cole, I think the drunks would've rushed me. Then what? The shot coming from you, Susan, was like an awakening . . . stopped everything without bloodshed. It must have brought sanity back to some of the men, because the crowd started breaking up."

At the house, Silas Kemp stepped back, aghast at the news. When Gabe, as usual, started to unhitch the team, Jesse waved him to the back. "I'll be out there in a bit." Then Kemp unhitched.

Jimmy had quit crying, but Jamie was still sobbing and all drawn up. Susan turned in great alarm to Jesse, and he took Jamie in his arms and they all went upstairs. Without delay Susan put Jamie to bed and sat by him, patting him reassuringly and speaking soothingly to him. "We're home, now, Jamie. We're home. . . . You're all right. Uncle Gabe is safe."

After some moments, Jamie stopped crying and looked into Susan's eyes.

"You're home, Jamie, Son," Susan said. "Uncle Gabe is safe."

Jimmy, his blue eyes big with concern, came over and patted Jamie, who smiled wanly. "You're all right, little brother," Jimmy assured him. "Nobody's gonna hurt you. I won't let them. You hear me, little brother?" And he kissed Jamie on the forehead.

"I think he wants to rest a while," Susan said, low.

Standing nearby, Jesse watched the boy for long moments. He was still such a thin little fellow, so heart-rending, although far from the shadow of the boy rescued in the Burro Mountains of New Mexico.

They were all patting and holding him now. Jamie stirred and closed his eyes and drifted off to sleep.

Susan murmured: "He's in shock from seeing someone he loved about to be murdered. Although it didn't happen, thank God, it brought back all the old horrors again."

"I guess drawing himself up was an instinctive way to ward it all off," Jesse said. "Poor kid. But he knows he's safe now."

They sat a while longer in troubled silence, until Jesse said in haste: "I'd better see about Gabe." Grabbing his last bottle of tequila, a shirt, and a bar of soap, he cast one look at the sleeping boy and hurried downstairs and out the rear of the house.

Gabe sat by the well, head down.

"Take a big slug of this," Jesse said, handing him the bottle.

Surprised, Gabe uncorked it, took a long pull, blinked, and coughed.

"Keep it," Jesse said. "Take a nip now and then. Come on. I'm going to fix you up."

As Jesse expected, there was still warm water in the side chamber of the wood-burning stove in the kitchen. He filled a large pan and took it outside and began washing and soaping Gabe down to his waist.

"Those drunks beat the hell out of you," Jesse deplored. "It's a good thing you're so strong. Might have killed a lesser man. I hope you got in some good punches?"

"Ah tried. Ah don't feel so strong now."

"You'll be sore as hell for some days. Rest will help." Gabe flinched as Jesse washed his torso. "Bruised ribs," Jesse said, probing a little. "But I don't think they're broken. If it's hurting real bad in the morning, we'd better wrap you." When he was finished, he gave Gabe the shirt.

"Thank you, Mistuh Jesse. You an' Miz Susan are so kind."

"You'd do the same or more for me. Maybe you'd better rest now. Susan and I will fix supper. I'll call you when it's ready. Save enough tequila for another day or two. . . . One more thing, Gabe. Don't go in town again by yourself. When we go in, you can come along."

Gabe nodded.

"This would happen just as you've found a nice lady friend. Sorry about that."

Gabe grinned like a gargoyle with his swollen features. "Ah reckon it's just as well, Mistuh Jesse. Ah didn't tell you she's married. Her husband's in Memphis."

"Why, Gabe, you rascal!"

At supper Gabe sat between the boys, while Jesse and Susan served and made a show of seeing that every little thing was done exactly right, drawing laughs with their comments and fancy flourishes with dishes and glasses. No one laughed harder than Gabe, who wept most of the time, grateful to be alive with friends.

Although little Jamie still looked pale and drawn, he was smiling and laughing with the others.

That night, while Gabe slept with the boys, Susan's mother ear caught no haunted cries of a small boy's tormented dreams.

Jesse loaded his Spencer carbine and took turns with Kemp as if on infantry guard duty. "We humiliated Ike Cole, so I expect to hear from him soon,"

Jesse confided to the veteran. "Next time I may have to kill him."

"Better carry a pistol in your waistband."

The soft Tennessee night passed quietly, yet replete with a foreboding Jesse could not put aside.

CHAPTER EIGHT

On the forenoon of the third day of the return to the home place, a trotting horse, smartly drawing a gleaming buggy, appeared at the far end of the drive as Jesse and Susan watched the boys busy at marbles. The driver was a proud and smiling B.L. Sawyer, beside him an excited and joyous young woman who couldn't stop waving both arms.

Jesse jumped up, shouting—"It's Mary Elizabeth!"—and dashed out to meet them.

When Sawyer had firmly reined in the spirited trotter, Jesse took his sister in his arms as she stepped down, saying through tears: "Brother Jesse . . . dear Brother Jesse. I'm so glad to see you at last."

Jesse was finding it difficult to get out a word. All he could do was hold her, and then he spoke her name and said—"My sweet little sister. It's been too long."—and embraced her again and again.

He stepped back to look at her, grown from the skinny youngster he'd left when the war had changed their lives, now an attractive young woman, stylishly dressed for travel. Under the little green hat an oval face with skin like porcelain and keenly alive eyes like blue chips. He continued to hold her as Gabe came out of nowhere to see to the horse after Sawyer stepped down.

Grasping his hand, Jesse said: "Thank you, sir. Thank you!"

"The stage came in early this morning, so why wait?"

"Mister Sawyer dropped everything to bring me out," Mary Elizabeth said. "I'm so grateful."

"After all, I am your family counselor," Sawyer teased her, assuming a serious expression.

"Indeed you are, sir." She laughed. "I won't let you get out of it, even if you try."

"Let's all go in," Jesse urged, picking up his sister's luggage.

Inside, the women embraced, and Mary Elizabeth said: "I feel I already know you, Susan, from what Jesse wrote me."

"It's so good to see you at last. We have longed for this. You are often in our thoughts. Jesse has told me about the nice things you sent him when he was in the Army, how he treasured your letters."

She made much of the boys, while mentioning no children of her own, her only reference to a family: "My husband Blair could not come with me, and sends his regrets. He's a busy tobacco farmer."

Susan showed them toward the parlor. Mary Elizabeth began gazing around in remembrance and speaking to Jesse about this and that. Both a bit solemn in their happiness.

After they had all sat for a few moments, Sawyer, as if he could no longer restrain himself, looked at

Susan and exclaimed: "The talk all around town is how with one shot you prevented a hanging. What amazing marksmanship that was. Ike Cole has hardly shown his face since then. . . . I've told Mary Elizabeth what happened."

"Oh, my goodness," Susan said, taken aback.

"It was simply a remarkable shot," Sawyer kept on.

"It was," Jesse agreed. "The same quick-acting snap shot I told you about when she got the ringleader of the deserters out West. Our friend Gabe Jackson is alive because of her."

Susan looked away. "Your little sister will think I'm a. . . ." She couldn't find the word.

". . . A very brave and resourceful person," Mary Elizabeth finished, and applauded loudly with Sawyer and Jesse, while, embarrassed, Susan looked down.

"And that fearless guardian of Petersburg's peace, Marshal Burdette, hadn't lifted a finger or said one word to stop it," Jesse spoke up, disgust rising in his voice. "I shamed him, and he said it was outside the city limits, which I doubt. He was there to enjoy the spectacle."

Sawyer nodded. "I'm not surprised."

"Gabe said he saw Ike Cole come out the rear of the saloon. Since when, counselor, did the city allow a saloon to stay open on Sunday?"

"The city fathers must not be aware, or they're just looking the other way."

"Burdette knows. As marshal, he should close it down. But maybe his whiskey is free."

"I think Burdette's days here are numbered. A tough element has taken root in town since the war, which he seems to ignore."

"There is one more matter concerning the marshal," Jesse said, looking at his sister in apology. "I don't want to take any more time away from your homecoming, but this is the first chance I've had to speak to Mister Sawyer about it." He explained to Sawyer what had happened to him in town concerning the Dougherty wagon.

"What was his response when you said you'd file a complaint if he tried to force you off the square again?" Sawyer asked.

"He didn't say anything . . . just stroked his mustache."

"Which only made you angrier. No man likes to be ignored. But rein in your feelings while in town. Ignore him, if you can. I'll be glad to write out a complaint if he bothers you again about parking the wagon."

"I appreciate that, sir."

Susan said: "Very shortly it will be time for an old-fashioned country dinner. And, of course, you are an honored guest with Mary Elizabeth, Mister Sawyer."

He made a courtly bow. "Thank you, dear lady."

"I realize we won't get you out our way very often. Jesse, will you please take sister's things upstairs? And, boys, go wash your hands."

"Yes, Mama," said Jimmy, glad to leave such boring adult talk. "Come on, Jamie."

"Yeah," Jamie said. Bright-eyed and happy, he was nothing like the fear-drawn little boy of a few days ago.

"There's so much to tell about the boys and what happened in Arizona," Susan said. "And before that Jesse's experiences in Mexico. Mary Elizabeth, your ears will be bent."

"I want to hear it all. Mister Sawyer has kept me informed on what's gone on here. Call me Mary or M.E., if you like. My name is somewhat long to say over and over."

Susan gave a little differing shake of her head. "I like Mary Elizabeth. It's sweet and goes 'way back."

"I agree," Sawyer said.

When Jesse came back, Susan left them for the kitchen to see how Gabe was progressing. Everything was ready. Since his rescue, he had spent more time than ever in the kitchen, plus helping around the house, as if he could not do enough.

Upon Susan's return to the parlor, Sawyer said: "I'd like to meet the man whose life you saved."

Hence, when they went into the dining room, Jesse waved Gabe over and said: Mister Sawyer, this is our good friend, Gabe Jackson."

Sawyer offered his hand at once and, as they shook, said: "I am mighty glad to meet you, Gabe. Thank God you're safe."

"Thank you, suh. Mistuh Jesse and Miz Susan saved me."

"That was a great shot she made."

"Yes, suh! Ah heard de shot an' saw de hangman's hat fly off. An' he jest slunk away. Nex' thing, Mistuh Jesse grabbed me down off de saddle an' hurried me fo' de wagon. An' dere stood Miz Susan with her pistol like an' angel sent down by de Lord."

Sawyer flashed Gabe a broad smile. "There's no better way to put it than that. Such a brave deed, and the danger to her around a bunch of drunks . . . if somebody had fired back. But fortunately they were taken by surprise."

At that moment Silas Kemp came in and Gabe returned to his duties and Jesse, turning to his sister, made the introductions. Kemp bowed.

"I know you're taking good care of everything, Mister Kemp," she said, extending her hand.

"I try to, Missus Somerville. I want to say that I appreciate having something to do, the way things are now, thanks to you and my friend, Mister Sawyer."

"While I'm here, we can have a good visit about the farm and what, if any, particulars need to be dealt with."

After lunch Mary Elizabeth excused herself to unpack and Jesse and Susan strolled back to the parlor with Sawyer.

"I realize you're wondering if your esteemed attorney at law has made any progress," he said with a smile of self-reproach. "My report is yes and no, which is about what I had expected at this stage. A Mister Randolph informs me that his client, now a candidate for the U.S. Senate on the Republican ticket, will agree only to a legal separation at this time . . . divorce is out of the question, he says."

Susan stamped her foot. "I knew it! He will never agree to a divorce unless forced. In his cruel way, he will delay and continue hurting me as long as he can. Meanwhile, even the slightest hint of any marital problems must be hushed during the election."

She was furious, close to weeping. Jesse put his arm around her. *Let her have her say. Let her get it out.*

"I detest the man!" she stormed. "In Tucson he wasn't even glad that Jimmy had been rescued, or that I was safe. I hoped I'd never see that man again, but now I know I must." In conclusion, she dropped her head.

Sawyer eased over and gently lifted her chin. "The fight has just begun, Susan. Absolutely there'll be no legal separation to please his royal highness. At the proper time, we're all going to Philadelphia to beard the lion in his den. Meantime, I'll inform Mister Randolph a legal separation is out of the question and point out that there is no political disgrace agreeing to an amicable divorce on the grounds of irreconcilable differences . . . that, in politics, his client will face greater problems than this, such as mud-slinging attacks on his character and the usual barbs from Democrats."

She began to relax a little, nodding at his logic.

"They'll refuse," Sawyer said. "Meanwhile, there is work to do before we leave. We'll go with all guns primed to fire . . . with an affidavit or two sworn before a notary." He looked straight into her eyes. "This old country lawyer is going to free you from all this, gallant, sure-shot lady."

CHAPTER NINE

In the cool of the evening Jesse and Silas Kemp sat in the living room, chatting in general about conditions around Petersburg and the war's lingering economic effects. A taciturn man by nature, Kemp was in a talkative mood tonight. The family was upstairs, getting further acquainted. Mary Elizabeth had brought a game and a picture book for Jimmy and Jamie, handmade handkerchiefs for Susan, and a bottle of aged Kentucky bourbon for Jesse.

He could see that she was greatly taken with the boys and they with her, now calling her Aunt Mary. It was regrettable, Jesse thought, that she had no little ones of her own. Thinking of her, he was conscious of a tremendous desire to protect and, somehow, contribute to her happiness. She also had lost much: both parents and brother Claiborne. She had married during the war. From what little Jesse knew about Blair Somerville, gleaned in her letters to him in the Army, Blair had come through middle Tennessee as an agent of the Confederacy buying cavalry mounts. So far, here, she had said very little about her husband, but Jesse guessed there was little or no reason to while visiting. She was obviously happy being with family in the old house where she had grown up.

Silas Kemp was saying: "Was up at Uriah Webb's this morning for eggs and milk and he said night riders are out again. He heard a farmer south of him aims to sell out. Got scared. Offered his place to Hanover in town, because he knows him, but Hanover couldn't take it. He's bought one place."

"I have no respect for Ike Cole, but he's the only real estate agent in town. Did the farmer go there?"

"Well, after Hanover, he did see Cole, who told the man if he couldn't find a buyer on his own, he'd see what he could do."

"Cole's on the look-out for business. The creepy bastard looks prosperous. Even asked me in town if the farm is up for sale. I told him no. That it wasn't mine to sell. That was before the hangin' attempt. I'm still shocked it came so close to happening. What if Susan and I hadn't chanced by at that time?"

The troublesome matter of the night riders died as if by mutual consent and for lack of more details, and presently Kemp said: "I don't hanker to bring up the war again, Jesse, but a lot of what happened back there is clearer now . . . and why it happened. I've talked to men who knew."

"Like what, Silas? Not being around, I've heard nothing, and really haven't minded it one bit. It took so much out of all of us. Including all my boyhood friends that enlisted here. John Hanover, for one, at Shiloh. Which is why his father hates me. I survived by wearing the hated blue out West. To be honest, I can understand why Mister Hanover feels that way. So tell me, Silas."

"To begin with, General Hood's physical condition. Did you know he had a withered arm from Gettysburg, and lost a leg at Chickamauga, amputated just a few inches from his hip? Had to be strapped to the saddle?"

"I didn't know about his arm. I'd heard about his leg. But you couldn't tell from the way he rode. He sat straight and proud."

"With all that, he must have been in pretty constant pain."

"Which could have affected his judgment at times."

Kemp nodded in turn. "When all he had for it was whiskey and laudanum."

"Makes you wonder at Franklin. All the charges we made. But in fairness to General Hood, no man fought harder, while Joe Johnston fought a defensive strategy. As men, we liked Johnston and admired Hood."

"Another thing about General Hood," Kemp said reflectively, "was the damnably bad luck that seemed to follow him in critical situations. I've heard it said that he had the chance to turn the Union flank at Gettysburg . . . early in the fighting . . . but the order never came through in the confusion."

"Silas, the South will be recalling the *buts* and *ifs* until kingdom come."

"I agree. But what I'm talking about is what happened at Spring Hill, or what was supposed to happen and didn't."

"I remember General Cheatham's corps crossed the Duck River on a pontoon bridge and we

marched on, feelin' good to be back on Tennessee
soil," Jesse said, warming to the subject. "East of us,
toward Columbia, we could hear our artillery
pounding away."

"That meant Hood had outflanked General
Schofield. He'd pulled a slick maneuver . . . faked
an attack at Columbia, held Schofield's attention
there while we went around. Then all Hood had to
do was take possession of the Franklin Pike at
Spring Hill and he had the Union Army bagged."

"What happened?"

"The story is that he ordered Cheatham to carry
that out, but it was never done."

Jesse said: "Camped that night, we could hear
wagons passing in the distance on the pike. We
were never ordered to the pike. There was a lot of
movement most of that night. I don't think those of
us in the ranks realized what we heard were Yankee
wagons . . . a whole damned army slipping by."

Kemp turned to fix his attention fully on Jesse.
"The story making the rounds now is that General
Cheatham spent that evening at the home of a certain doctor's wife, when he should have been carrying out Hood's orders."

Jesse sat back, struck dumb.

"The same lady whose jealous husband had shot
and killed General Earl Van Dorn earlier in the
war," Silas explained. "In the bedroom or the parlor
seems unclear. For Cheatham's sake, the husband
must have been absent."

"Hey! That's quite a story, Silas. And what gets a
man is that the slaughter at Franklin could have
been avoided if Schofield had been cut off. Instead,

he hurried on and entrenched. Oh, a sharp fight at the pike would've followed, but nothing like us charging breastworks late next day." Jesse groaned. "Yes, Hood was unlucky as hell and so were the rest of us Johnny Rebs. This gets back to what plagued us all during the war . . . poor staff work. Poor communications. At Franklin, we didn't coordinate our attacks, so they'd stop one, then brace for the next one. In your opinion, Silas, what was Hood's biggest mistake at Franklin?"

"He should have waited for his artillery to come up. But who knows? Or he should've tried to outflank Schofield. Or he should have held back. Not attacked at all, the way it was. But Hood was always the fighter. . . . And I'll never forget seeing our dead generals laid out on the back gallery of the McGavock mansion next day. I remember my general, Pat Cleburne, had on a bloody white shirt and a new uniform. He was in his sock feet. His boots had been stolen during the night, with his watch and sword belt. Someone said his body had been found about fifty yards from the breastworks."

"He was one of the best," Jesse said.

"Well liked as an officer. He asked as much of himself as he did his men."

They let the silence settle around them and said no more, because there was no more to be said tonight. Jesse hated to think the terrible losses at Franklin had been for nothing, but the thought would always persist. When Kemp stirred to leave, Jesse said—"Wait. We're going to have a drink."— and he went upstairs.

Finding the boys playing with the game and the

women chatting like sisters gave him a welcome feeling of returning to another reality.

"We're catching up on some things," Susan greeted him.

"And we're just getting started," Mary Elizabeth said. "I'm enjoying you-all so much."

"We're mighty happy to have you with us," he said. "Silas and I have been talking. Now we're going to have a drink of that good bourbon you brought me."

They had that drink, then they had another. They knew that the war would never die.

With the boys finally in bed, the adults stayed up and talked. At Susan's urging, Jesse told how first Jamie, then Jimmy, had been rescued from the Apache camp in New Mexico. And Susan explained how she had gone about locating Jesse after reading about him in the newspapers. He noticed that his sister, although often smiling and always pleasant, contributed very little about her life in Kentucky. It was late when she kissed them good night and went to the bedroom next to the boys.

The wind was up and the old house creaked and a shutter was banging at the end of the hall, adding to Jesse's mood after his conversation with Kemp. Sleep still eluded him as Susan lay in his arms after their good-night kisses.

"I'm restless, too," she murmured in his ear.

"Silas and I got to thinking about the war. He told me a lot I didn't know. What he's heard from veterans close to General Hood's command. Main thing, what happened at Franklin would've been avoided if an order to close the pike at Spring Hill had been carried out, blocking the Union forces from going on to Franklin to entrench."

"Why wasn't it carried out?"

"That's where the plot thickens. There's a woman involved."

"Oh, a *femme fatale?*"

"In reverse, General Cheatham called on her. At least, that's the story."

"And so?"

"We had the Battle of Franklin."

After a little, she said: "I'm worried about Mary Elizabeth. I hate to tell you, but I fear she's in an unhappy marriage."

"What?" he was startled.

"She didn't come right out and say as much. Nothing she said directly. It was what I sensed . . . her loneliness. Her affection for the boys. And when they hug her or ask questions, she is so loving and sweet and understanding. No mother could be kinder and knowing. They enjoy calling her Aunt Mary, which delights her. She wants children. Apparently Blair Somerville doesn't."

"Why wouldn't a man want children?"

"Not all people do. It's a responsibility. Maybe they just don't want to be bothered."

"You're wiser than I am, Susan. I take pleasure in watching ours grow up, and some of the antics they pull."

"But not all men are like you. And not all families have a Gabe Jackson to love the children and see after them and entertain them."

"We are mighty fortunate. I realize that. Gabe is an exceptional man."

Susan seemed to be weighing her thoughts before

she spoke again. "Mary Elizabeth is unhappy for another reason without saying so. Blair appears to have a roving eye. He is gone a lot. Often for several days at a time."

"Well, I'll be damned."

"As pretty and sweet as she is."

"I was in camp at Atlanta when she wrote and said she had married. I wrote back and wished her happiness. I think she got lonely, which I can understand. I believe he's some years older. Now she may want to leave him."

"She gave no indication of that."

"Be hard to say. Well, I won't say a word about this unless she brings it up. On the other hand, maybe I should come right out and ask her if she's unhappy. She's my dear sister, and I'm going to protect her. She needs to stay with us a while . . . needs family around her. She can go back to Arizona with us, if she wants to."

"I've had the same thought."

He frowned. "It also gets complicated. May have to call on B. L. Sawyer again. Well, for now, she's here with us, and that's what matters."

Then they slept.

Several hours later, something broke into Jesse's sleep. Not the rise and fall of the wind or the loose shutter. A different intrusion. A drumming that roused old danger signals within him: the sound of horses coming at a hard run on the drive leading to the house.

"Stay here," he said as he slid out of bed, heading for his Spencer in the corner of the room. Another moment and he heard shots and a splatter of bullets striking the house, and then the riders were swiftly gone, their hoof beats fading fast. He thought: *A small bunch.*

Down the hallway he found the kids stirring and Mary Elizabeth sleepily asking: "What is it?"

"It's all right now," he assured her.

By then Susan was at his side, and they began getting everybody back to their bedroom.

"I'm going downstairs to check on Silas," Jesse said.

"Don't go outside," Susan warned.

He went down, calling for Silas, and found him at the open front door.

"I heard 'em comin'. Got a look after they fired an' went by."

"Silas, you know better'n that. What if they'd fired with you at the door?"

"I said *after*, didn't I?"

"How many riders you think?"

"Six or eight. Dressed in white."

Jesse heard Gabe calling for him. He went outside, yelling for him to come to the house, that everybody was all right.

"Dey rode past de cabins," Gabe reported. "Nevah fired."

Daylight revealed no damage except the siding of the house pockmarked with scattered bullet holes

Kemp dug out a bullet and held it for Jesse to see. "Looks like a carbine slug," he said. "Don't figure they'd tote muzzleloaders on horseback."

While Gabe fixed breakfast for the family, Jesse and Kemp took off on the trail left by the riders. The arid ground told them very little. But in the softer footing of a little brook still dry from summer, they found one print with a bar across the shoe.

"Sometimes a bar shoe is good for a sore-footed horse," Jesse said. "Something a horseman would try."

The trail led eastward from the house and vanished some two miles farther

"We could learn more if we had horses," Jesse said. "Cut a wide swath, back and forth. Everything's mighty dry at this time of year."

"Now where would they keep horses and robes?" Kemp pondered.

"At the edge of town."

"Yeah. The robes could be just long white shirts they roll up in saddlebags."

As they started back, Jesse said: "From what B. L. Sawyer told us, when we came, the Klan, besides keeping blacks in place, seemed to be concerned with public morals. A man in another county was flogged for chasing another man's wife. Ike Cole fits the part about terrorizing blacks, but would the Klan hang Gabe Jackson for not tipping his hat? Seems too far out to me, even for them. . . . Ike Cole fails to fit as a defender of public morals because he has none himself. Just a low-class white man who feeds his vanity by preying on defenseless blacks and has a like following in town."

"On top of that, he's a real estate agent. Wouldn't surprise me if he's not behind the whole damned thing," Kemp said flatly.

"You're echoing what I've come to think. But prove it."

They found the women in a high state of concern.

"It's more of what's been going on, a scare to get

farmers to sell out," Jesse explained. "Somebody wants this farm. Or maybe Ike Cole's getting back at us. Silas and Gabe and I'll keep watch tonight, but I don't look for 'em to come again soon. They have to figure we'll be on guard. Now, Silas and I sure would appreciate some breakfast."

Afterward, while the lads played, Mary Elizabeth said: "I'd sell the place in a minute, now that you've said you don't want it, Jesse. If you did, I'd give it to you."

He gave her a little pat. "I know you would, though that would be more than I should accept. But you understand that our home is in Arizona?"

"Yes. And it's so far away."

Seeing the look on her face, he said at once: "Silas might be a good buyer for you. He's a good, honest. A hard worker. With backing to help him get started, he could put in crops and raise stock and pay the place out."

"I really hadn't thought that far. All I've been doing is enjoying myself."

"Susan and I and the boys want you to. Every minute while you're here."

"Well, about Silas. I'll think about it. Why, yes!"

Jesse reflected hard for a moment about what he wished to say and how to say it, then, with a glance at Susan, he said: "We don't want to interfere in your life, Mary Elizabeth. We just want you to feel happy and secure. When everything is settled in Philadelphia, and here, too, I should say, would you like to live with us in Arizona?"

Her pretty face crumbled. "Oh, Brother Jesse, you must be reading my mind. I've been so happy here. I love you all so much."

"Yes, make your home with us," Susan said. "We all love you very much."

And then they both held her and she was softly crying and there were no dry eyes, and Jesse knew the Wilder family was one again.

CHAPTER TEN

Thereafter, Jesse and Kemp and Gabe posted themselves around the house at night. But the riders did not return, and Jesse and Susan agreed that early Saturday would be a good time to drop by with Mary Elizabeth and visit Nancy Mason and her boys and her father. Also, on the chance Mr. Sawyer would be in his office, Jesse wanted to bring their friend up to date.

Although Petersburg was busy on trade day, it wasn't like she remembered, Mary Elizabeth observed a bit sadly.

"Our old town has shrunk," Jesse said. "It'll take some years for it to recover from the war and the people it's lost. But I think it will in time."

Nancy greeted them graciously, and she and Mary Elizabeth soon connected on their school days, while the boys rushed outside to play on the swing. John Sutton wasn't in, so Jesse excused himself to walk downtown, hoping to see Sawyer.

As he started down the street, caution suddenly

gripped him and he went back to the wagon for his pistol, which he stuck inside his waistband. In the folds of his shirt, it was visible but not, he thought, in a public way. He was not showing off. He was being discreet. After all that had happened, instinct warned him to protect himself. What if he ran into Ike Cole and his drunks? Burdette was another threat, ever bent on harassing him. Jesse sensed a perverse, unstable will in the man to dominate around the square, his bailiwick for years, made worse now by drinking. Further, Jesse had belittled him before others at the lynching party. It would be wise if he could avoid the marshal today.

He drew no more than a few glances as he made his way to the square. No staring. He recognized no one. Burdette was talking loudly to a group in front of the general store, gesturing as he blew.

Seeing Miss Pringle fussing over papers on her desk, Jesse went in. She seemed surprised to see him, and, upon his entry, said: "Mister Sawyer is out of town until Monday. This is a good day for me to catch up. Is there anything I can do for you, Mister Wilder?"

"I came by to bring him up to date. We had robed riders the other night at the farm . . . shot into the house and rode on. Fortunately nobody was wounded."

She put a hand to her lips in shock. "Oh, Mister Wilder."

"They haven't come back. Silas Kemp and I are prepared, if they do."

"It's sad, what's happening here. The riff-raff we have now. A near hanging. Country people in fear, some selling out. Mister Sawyer is still talking about the marvelous shot your wife made to break up that mob."

"There's another way to look at it. She also saved Ike Cole's life. I was ready to shoot him." He turned toward the door. "We're all visiting at Nancy Mason's today. Marshal Burdette is up the street. I'd like to avoid him. Guess Mister Sawyer has told you why?"

"Yes. By the way, the city council will be discussing the marshal at the next meeting. He may be on his way out, after lording it over the square for years. Mister Sawyer has told councilmen how Burdette keeps hounding you, forcing you to park your passenger wagon at the old yard. And how did it happen that your mules were led way off? Oh, there've been other complaints. Petersburg has never had a lynching. Why didn't he stop Ike Cole? People think he favors that rough bunch. Or is he afraid of them? And he spends a lot of the city's time loafing at the saloon. It's been a build up of things."

She stopped all at once. "Whew! I'm talking too much. Please be careful, Mister Wilder. I'll tell Mister Sawyer you called. I'm so sorry you've had so much trouble."

"Thank you, Miss Pringle. I just hope we can avoid any more here, and that we can get on to Philadelphia and straighten out our lives."

He left the office and paused on the boardwalk to look around. More people on the square now. Burdette was still blowing. Jesse debated whether to go over and say a quick hello to Mrs. Balmer, then told himself he'd better get back.

As he started across the street, a now familiar grating voice shouted: "Hold on, Wilder!" Jesse realized that Burdette had seen him go into the office and was waiting for him to come out.

"What is it, Marshal?" Jesse asked in a calm voice, walking toward Burdette to get out of the way of a passing buggy. He willed himself to avoid trouble, if at all possible.

As Burdette strode forcefully toward him, big pistol wobbling on his belt as usual, Jesse saw that he was a little unsteady on his feet.

"You'll have to hand over that pistol you're packin'," Burdette ordered in a slurred voice.

Astonished, Jesse all but shouted: "What?"

"I said hand over your pistol."

Shoppers were stopping to gawk.

Speaking slowly and emphatically in an effort to cool this, Jesse said: "Give up my pistol, when just a few days ago Ike Cole and his bunch tried to hang my old family friend not far from here? And just two nights ago white-robed riders shot up my family farmhouse?"

"It's against a city ordinance to wear a gun in public."

"I have the right to defend my family and self. It's in the Constitution, if you've ever read it?"

"Don't pull any of that book-learnin' stuff on me, Wilder. The law has to be enforced in town."

"Then close the back door of the saloon on Sunday! That's where Ike Cole and his drunks got their whiskey when they tried to hang my friend."

"That's a lie!"

"My friend saw Ike Cole come out the back door."

"A nigger's word!"

"The words of a freeman, Marshal. First, Cole's bunch took him off to a barn and beat 'im up. They were all drinking."

"As for the hangin' attempt, that was outside the city limits."

"It would have been murder, Marshal. Why didn't you stop it?"

"Don't tell me what's right . . . you . . . you damned blue-coat!"

Burdette was starting to bluster, which Jesse knew was a dangerous sign. Jesse turned, thinking just to walk away from this. But Burdette's voice caught him.

"Surrender your gun!"

"I refuse because it would leave me defenseless after all that's happened to me and my family."

"By Gawd, yuh will!"

Jesse saw it in Burdette's reddish eyes, in the way he stiffened, hands lifting, weaving. Half drunk, furious, his authority questioned in public, he was going to draw his pistol. Two quick steps and Jesse caught Burdette's right arm clearing the holster. Although the marshal was paunchy, he was a powerful man and they struggled back and forth on the boardwalk for the weapon, Burdette's whiskey breath foul in Jesse's face. Nearby onlookers backed away, shouting alarm. A woman screamed.

Burdette grunted when the pistol, pointed skyward, went off. He seemed surprised at the roar. As Jesse felt the other's grip loosen, he wrestled the pistol free and yelled into Burdette's now-startled face: "Why, damn you! You would've shot me over this! You're drunk!"

Burdette just stood there slackly, features enveloped in a kind of daze.

Quickly, but with grim deliberation, Jesse cleared all the chambers with the ejector rod and returned the pistol, handle first, saying: "Here's your pistol, Marshal. Now, quit hounding me every time I come to town."

Then Jesse turned and walked unhurriedly through the gaping bystanders, filled with disgust, yet thankful he had not been forced to shoot Burdette in self-defense. He sensed that he might have to yet. This was not the end; it wasn't over. It struck him that the marshal, drunk, was slow on the draw.

He said nothing at the house about the run-in, and the enjoyable visiting continued past four o'clock. Heading out, he was relieved that Burdette wasn't in sight. The square was virtually deserted.

They were beyond town when he turned to Susan and said: "I hate to tell this after the fine afternoon we've all had at Nancy's, but Burdette tried to make me surrender my pistol when I went downtown."

She sat a little straighter and became very still, blue-green eyes wide. "I see it's still in the wagon. What did you do?"

He told her what had happened.

"Why does he persist?"

"He thinks it makes him look good as a lawman. And he can continue to hound me because I'm a pariah to many people. Through him they can vent their feelings over the war. He called me a blue-coat today. It's popular to do that."

"He's a despicable man and I fear for you, Jesse."

"I can take care of myself most times."

"From now on somebody must be with you when you go to the square for *any* reason. Either me or Silas."

"I don't think it would have made any difference today."

Mary Elizabeth broke in: "Susan's right, Jesse. Or I will."

"Well, we'll see."

"Don't talk like that," Susan said.

Soon they reached the house. Silas Kemp was sitting on the porch in the restless manner of a person who'd been waiting for them. Gabe waved and took care of the team.

"I've got news," Kemp said. "Samuel Hill's called a meeting at his place early tomorrow afternoon about the night riders. Uriah Webb told me. Think we should go, Jesse?"

"I do. Not that I'll be welcome."

CHAPTER ELEVEN

A few farmers were still arriving when Jesse and Kemp reached Samuel Hill's home. It was an impressive three-story residence, with white columns and a long porch. Its air of well-being reminded Jesse of some he'd seen on plantations in the deep South. Kemp parked his wagon and they stood beside it.

Jesse wondered what Hill thought he could accomplish here today. What could any of them? Some thirty or so had come. A face or two seemed vaguely familiar. His father had rarely been one to invite neighbors over or to drop by on others. These men were middle-aged or older, mostly past the age of having served in the war. Over by the porch Uriah Webb was in earnest conversation with Hill and two others.

Mr. Samuel Hill, Jesse mused, his mind flashing back. *A prominent slave owner before the war and a fire-eating Secessionist who would actually begin to froth at the mouth when discussing Abolitionists and black Republicans. Known for having said . . . "The South can fight her own battles, and, if she can't do it inside the Union, by God, she can damn' well do it outside the Union!"*

Hill, as a member of the Lost Creek school board, had hired one Jesse Wilder, an honor graduate of the Nashville Academy, for the schoolteacher's job at thirty-five dollars a month.

Jesse had chanced to meet Hill on the road home that painful day after being mustered out of the Union Army of the West. Except for a slight jerk at sight of Jesse, Hill had trotted past him without a sign of recognition, staring straight ahead.

Now Jesse saw Hill nod to Webb and mount the stone steps to the porch. He stood there, looking over the gathering, an impressive man of large frame and heavy girth, a strong, heavy face and a white beard that fell to his chest. He raised his right hand and spoke in a voice that went with his size. "I thank you good neighbors for coming. You know why we're here." A faint glint of amusement crossed his face. "Question is what can we do about it?"

"Somethin' will break," a farmer near Jesse said. "They'll make a mistake. When they do, by grab, we'll make 'em pay. My wife is plumb scared at night. I keep a shotgun by the front door."

An angry voice added: "They shot up my house, gunned down my milk cow as they rode off."

Another man said: "My wife wants me to sell out. Move into town. At my age, I'm tempted."

"Aw, Jim," one joked, "who's gonna buy that ol' rundown farm?"

"I understand there's a banker at Lewisburg that's

bought some places. I've got his name right here. It's
J. C. Phelps. At the First National. He sends a man
down to appraise and make an offer."

"What've the offers been like?"

"Low, they say."

"Way things are you'd expect that. And when
times get better, that banker will sell off and get hog
fat. He can afford to wait until they do."

"Remember this, neighbors," Hill said. "It's not
going to stay like this. One problem now is lack of
help. I don't have but one nigger left here. I dare say
a lot of you are in the same fix, or worse."

"Well, there's two reasons for that, Sam. Freed
niggers went to the big towns lookin' for work.
What didn't go when the war ended, these night riders have scared off, a whole passel of 'em."

"My advice to you men is don't rush to sell out.
Of course, circumstances may force you to . . . that's
different. I'm not going to sell. Where would the
missus and me go? I want to die in this old house.
Land prices will come back. So will prices for farm
products."

"But when? Corn's no higher now than it was two
years ago."

"True. But look at it this way. Land prices will sta-
bilize once we shut down these night riders. I urge
you to hold on. Don't rush to sell out."

"Shore easier said than done, Mister Sam. How
we gonna do that?"

"Yeah, Mister Sam. Tell us."

Hill threw them a broad smile. "As you men
know, I wasn't in our revered Army of Tennessee.
Too blamed old. I know you-all have rifles and

shotguns. It seems to me the first order of business is to get organized. Did any of you serve in the Army?"

A hand went up. "I was in Joe Wheeler's cavalry for a year, till I was wounded."

"Anybody else?"

"I was in the militia for a while. Never fired a shot."

No one else spoke.

They stirred restlessly, not knowing where to start, and looked at one another in frustration.

Jesse hadn't wanted to get into this, sensing how he probably would be greeted. He gave Kemp an urging look, but Kemp said: "With all you've been through, why don't you try something to help 'em get organized?"

Still Jesse hesitated.

"Somebody speak up," Hill said.

As Hill looked his way, Jesse lifted a hand. "Mister Hill, I would like to suggest, for a start, your farm be made headquarters and you appoint several men to direct operations in certain sections, yourself included." Although these were only general suggestions about getting started, Jesse realized he could appear to be currying favor with a man who regarded him as a virtual traitor.

An agitated expression came over Hill's face. He sent Jesse a blunt look, and said: "I don't think we need any suggestions from a man who disgraced the Confederacy and his good family name by wearing the Union uniform in the West. I'm surprised, sir, that you have the gall to show up at a public meeting."

Everybody turned to stare at Jesse. Some nodded. All seemed to take in his features in detail.

He felt no surprise, for he had known what would happen if he spoke up. Yet something must be said to get them moving. And in a distinct, controlled voice, feeling suddenly this was also the best chance he'd ever have to state his side and gain understanding, he said: "Mister Hill, I want you and all the neighbors here today to get the straight of what happened to me in the war and later. I ask your considerate attention. I served in the Army of Tennessee from Shiloh through Franklin, where I was wounded. I woke up in a Yankee hospital in Nashville, by mistake, I'm sure. As I recovered, I was sent to Camp Morton, a hellhole of a prison in Indiana. Men were dying like flies. Service in the Union Army out West was dangled before me. I refused it as a way out. But as time went on, to save my life, I volunteered for duty on the frontier. And, yes, I felt like the lowest of traitors. Hundreds of other Johnny Rebs did the same. We fought Indians, guarded wagon trains, and did post duty. But we never fired one shot against the South. There was *no way* they could force us to do that. Besides, that had been agreed when we volunteered. Too, the Yankees were short of men out there."

His throat was dry. He stopped to swallow. Every face was turned toward him, engrossed. Even Hill and Webb.

"After almost two years, we were mustered out to return to our homes in disgrace. That was the price we paid for survival. But we are still Southerners."

He swallowed again and went on. "I understand how Mister Hill feels, and I can understand how you men may feel. But I bear no grudge against Mister Hill for what he said. Nor will I against you. All I ask is for your understanding."

He changed tone, speaking faster. "The other night robed riders shot into the Wilder farmhouse. Luckily no one was hurt among my family that includes my wife and two children, as well as my sister. Nor was Silas Kemp or myself. Silas, who is looking after the place, was sleeping downstairs and got a glimpse of the bunch as they rode off. Some six or eight riders. . . . Next morning, on foot, we followed their trail till it faded out. Not much to see. We did find the print of one bar shoe. You don't see many bar shoes. We pass that on to you. Silas is here with me today. He served in the Army of Tennessee through Nashville. We'll help if you say so."

An awkward silence seemed to follow. No one spoke. Hill regarded Jesse without a change of expression, and the others shuffled a little uneasily and turned to the porch, as if waiting for Hill or somebody there to say something.

Jesse slipped back beside Kemp, realizing it was time to go, thankful he'd had this one chance to tell his story at a public gathering. Not one man had shouted or cursed him.

"I'm glad you said what you did," Kemp said as they drove down the road. "There's nothing like the hard truth. You spoke from the heart. I believe there'll be a better understanding now."

"Thanks, Silas. I hope so. I feel a great relief. I

needed to say it. It was like a confession, and they say confession is good for the soul."

At the house Gabe was playing with the children in the yard while the women watched. A harried-looking Susan hastened out to meet them. "Don't unhitch yet. Mister Sawyer just left with word that Marshal Burdette has filed a complaint against you in court for carrying a gun in public. It comes up Tuesday."

Jesse felt himself smiling. "I almost feel like laughing. I'm not surprised. But I wonder why he hasn't filed on me for taking his pistol and unloading it. That's more serious."

"It's not a laughing matter, Jesse. It's just another way to get at you. Mister Sawyer wants you to come in today and talk to him."

"Glad to. I look at it this way, Susan . . . it gives us an opening. What we've needed. I'm going to ask Mister Sawyer to write up complaints against Burdette for forcing me to move the wagon and the mules being led off. I want to throw this right back at the marshal."

"I'll take you in," Kemp obliged. "We'll park where you can walk right across to Sawyer's office. You won't need a gun today."

"After dinner," Jesse said.

Susan insisted on going with them. They parked below the square and walked to Sawyer's office without seeing Burdette. Jesse urged Kemp to go with them. Ms. Pringle showed them in.

Sawyer greeted them with an exaggerated— "You'd better get in here, Jesse Wilder."—spoke warmly to Kemp, then made a point of escorting Susan to a chair. When all were seated, he said: "If this weren't so serious and downright mean-spirited, I'd treat it with little concern. But the marshal is after you, Jesse, while appearing to stay within the law. There is an ordinance of long standing against carrying a gun in public, going back to when a few hotheads would shoot it out in town. During the war most men went armed. Since then, very few, and, if done in a quiet, unobtrusive manner, nothing was said until this. As a matter of fact, I don't recall a single instance of a man being fined for going armed in public." He frowned in disapproval. "Now this. We shall contest to our utmost. You'd better tell me all about it, Jesse," he said, preparing to take notes.

Jesse did.

Sawyer looked up from his scribbling. "That all?"

"I'd riled him when I asked why he hadn't tried to stop the lynching . . . which he claimed was outside the city limits . . . and why he hadn't closed the back door of the saloon that Sunday. I told him that was how Ike Cole and his bunch got their whiskey when they tried to hang Gabe."

"I may ask you to testify to same, Jesse. However, by a strict interpretation of the ordinance, you'll likely be fined."

"Be worth it."

"The justice of the peace is Theodore Americus Cooper. A retired attorney, respected, about my age. A bit officious and political. But a good, fair-minded man. He's what is needed in that position, handling touchy matters." Sawyer regarded him keenly, appraising Jesse. "Is there something else?"

"There is. Susan and I have agreed on this. I wish to file a harassment complaint against Burdette for forcing me to move our Dougherty passenger wagon from below the square to the old wagon yard. Also, the mule team was led off to a distant pasture and left."

"About how far from the wagon yard is the pasture where you found the mules?"

"A good mile. Richard and Tim Mason pointed out the direction the men had taken the mules, and went with me down the road."

"Did they know the men?"

"No, sir. Neither did a gentleman, working out in his yard, who saw the men pass and wondered what was up."

"But Marshal Burdette was not one of the two men who took the mules?"

"He was not."

"That weakens our case. Did you question Burdette about the matter?"

"I did, when I got back. I asked him to investigate who had taken the mules. He just scoffed. Said it was just a prank. Nothing to investigate. I told him it was an effort to put me on foot, and if I had come upon the two taking the mules, I would've considered it theft. I also told him that if he tried once more to force me to move the wagon to the yard, I'd ask you to draw up a complaint against him for public harassment."

"Better tell me more about the Doughtery as a passenger wagon."

"Well, sir, it has side doors, and there's an iron step plate you use to get in. It has two seats behind the driver's seat, a permanent roof, like a stagecoach, and canvas side curtains that can be rolled up or strapped down in rough weather. And there's a boot in back, a chain-supported platform for baggage, like a coach. It's roomy and comfortable for a wagon, ideal for a family like ours."

"I should think so, with protection from the elements."

"Burdette insisted it was a freight wagon and couldn't be parked anywhere around the square. I explained that the Doughtery was a passenger wagon and not used to carry supplies. That on the Western frontier it was also used as an ambulance. He said that didn't matter, it was the size of a freight wagon. Move it or face a fine. To appease him, I moved it to the yard, walked back to town, and did my shopping."

"I'll draw this up," Sawyer said, "and we'll present it to the court. I will inform Judge Cooper before court opens that we have a complaint against the marshal. Burdette's will be heard first."

On Tuesday Kemp drove Jesse and Susan into town for a ten o'clock appearance in court. Jesse was not armed.

"I still have my pistol in my purse," Susan said when they left the house. "God forbid that I'd have to use it again."

"God forbid that you wouldn't have it if needed again," Jesse said gently, his arm around her.

Sawyer's manner was confident and reassuring when they showed up in his office. "I never go into a case I don't expect to win. I intend to make Burdette back off about the size of your passenger wagon." He took them to the other side of the square to a low, frame building adjacent to a two-story building bearing the designation of CITY HALL.

"Wait in the courtroom while I go next door and inform his honor what we'll have." He smiled and nodded approvingly. "Protocol must be observed. A clerk in the business office acts as bailiff."

He returned shortly, and they all waited. Burdette came in, nodded, and sat beyond them. Jesse surmised he was sober today.

Promptly at ten o'clock, Judge Theodore Americus Cooper entered from the city hall side, preceded by a mousy-looking little man, who raised both hands and spoke in a surprisingly clear voice: "Everybody stand for the Honorable Judge Cooper."

All stood.

An erect, heavy-bodied man in a dark blue suit, Cooper had a flowing mane of white hair and full beard to go with an air of dignity and the impression therein of much legal knowledge. He went to what served as the bench, a common table with a gavel.

"Please be seated," he said in a formal voice, and looked at a paper the bailiff placed before him. "Marshal Burdette, I see your complaint is first. You have charged Mister Jesse Wilder with carrying a gun in public, in violation of Ordinance Fifty-Six on October Seventh. In addition, that the defendant, Mister Wilder, seized your pistol when you ordered him to surrender his."

"What does the defense have to say?"

Sawyer stood and said: "Your honor, the defendant does not deny that he was armed that day. He was wearing a pistol inside his waistband for protec-

tion, which he will explain. And he had not strolled
about the square, showing off. He had walked to my
office from the Nancy Mason home where he and
his family were visiting. I wasn't in, and he left and
started back for the Mason home, when Marshal
Burdette stopped him. At this point, I should like to
question Mister Wilder on what followed."

"Proceed, Mister Sawyer."

Jesse stood, and Sawyer said: "Describe what occurred next."

"I went over to the marshal and he demanded that
I surrender my pistol. I refused and explained that I
needed it for my family's protection after two recent
events. My wife and I had prevented Ike Cole and
his bunch from lynching an old family friend, a free-
man. My wife stopped it by shooting off Ike Cole's
hat. Fortunately there was a pistol in her purse. I
myself was prepared to shoot Cole, if he persisted,
having taken my gun from the wagon. Then a few
nights later, robed riders shot up the Wilder farmhouse, but no one was injured. Silas Kemp and I
tried to track them next morning, but lost their
trail." Jesse paused. "The marshal still demanded
my gun. I noticed that he had been drinking. He was
unsteady on his feet."

"That's a lie, Judge!" Burdette shouted, leaping to
his feet. "I wasn't drinkin'!"

"Did you see Marshal Burdette take a drink, Mister Wilder?" Cooper asked.

"No, sir. I did not. But he was unsteady."

"Then that is conjecture. Proceed with your testi-
mony."

"We had more words. Again he demanded I surrender my pistol. Again I refused. When he started to draw his pistol, I feared he would shoot me, unless I obeyed. So I grabbed his arm. We wrestled. The pistol discharged once, straight up. I grabbed it free, accused him of trying to kill me and of being drunk. Then I emptied all the chambers, returned his pistol, told him to quit hounding me every time I came to town, and walked away."

"Aw, I wasn't goin' to shoot him, Judge," Burdette said in a belittling way. "I was just tryin' to force him to surrender his pistol and obey the law."

Cooper let the matter rest briefly, then looked at Sawyer. "Does the defense have anything further to bring out on this?"

"No, Your Honor. Mister Wilder has said it all. However, at this time Mister Wilder wishes to lodge a complaint of continued harassment against Marshal Burdette regarding the forced removal of his Doughtery passenger wagon from near the square to the old wagon yard. And the removal of his team of mules from the yard to a distant pasture about a mile away without his knowledge, apparently done to leave him afoot. I now ask Mister Wilder to describe in detail what happened that day."

Jesse nodded to Sawyer, then the judge, and described the Doughtery to the court.

"I was goin' by the size of the wagon, Judge," Burdette said at once. "It's a big 'un."

"None the less," Cooper said to Jesse, "you did move the Doughtery to the old wagon yard."

"Yes, sir," Jesse began, and he explained the circumstances surrounding the missing mules and the finding of them. It came to Jesse that in the heat of his feelings he was speaking too fast. More deliberately, he continued, concluding: "In view of his complaint against me today, I decided to file the harassment complaint."

Cooper turned to Burdette. "What is your reply to the harassment complaint, Marshal?"

"I deny it, Judge. I was just tryin' to do my duty and enforce the law for the good citizens of Petersburg."

"You assumed that the Dougherty passenger wagon was a freight wagon?"

"Yes, Judge, because of its size."

"How do you account for the mules being led off?"

"Well, sir, there were people listening in to our argument. I figger some of them led the mules off. It was a prank. Nothin' else."

Cooper turned to Sawyer. "Counsel?"

"Your Honor, it is Mister Wilder's contention that the mules being led away, where he likely would not have located them that day, was a continuation of the marshal's harassment. Now I shall ask Mister Wilder to state that in his own words. Mister Wilder, please address the court."

"Thank you and Judge Cooper. I believe that when I walked back to town from the yard to do my shopping, Marshal Burdette told his cohorts to lead the mules off. Word had to have been passed for that to happen in such a short time."

"That's a blasted lie!" Burdette shouted, waving his arms, squaring around at Jesse.

Cooper pounded the table with the gavel. "Order! Order! Mister Burdette, the court now gives you the opportunity to reply in a proper manner."

"Thank you, Judge. I had nothin' to do with the mules bein' led off. I didn't pass any word. The whole thing had to be a prank, because Wilder

served in the Yankee Army out West. Folks here
know what he did . . . how he disgraced us all. They
were standin' around listenin' to us argy about the
wagon. Takin' the mules off was their way to get
back at him. It was a prank, Judge, pure and simple." He stepped back with a gloating look at Jesse.

"Your Honor," Sawyer said evenly, "Marshal Burdette's remarks about Mister Wilder's service in the
Union Army are uncalled for here. But in reference
to the matter at hand, it is rather curious that the
mules were moved while Mister Wilder was shopping. We believe word was passed to get it done to
greatly and further inconvenience my client."

Burdette said no more.

After a thoughtful interval, Judge Cooper said:
"There are extenuating circumstances in both complaints. Mister Wilder had recently gone through
two violent situations. He was armed that day in
town, but was not making a show of it. The court
must consider what he would have done had he run
into Ike Cole when he went downtown to the office
of Mister Sawyer. In his intention to do the right
thing, Marshal Burdette was wrong about the
Dougherty passenger wagon being a freight wagon.
I have seen the Dougherty wagon myself in
Nashville. But there is no evidence he passed word
for the mules to be moved. The argument between
Mister Wilder and Marshal Burdette was loud. It
must have drawn the attention of bystanders. Any of
them could have led the mules off while Mister
Wilder was shopping." Judge Cooper paused and
regarded all parties. "Therefore, it is the decision of
the court that all complaints be dismissed, with the
provision that, in the future, in town, Mister Wilder

wear a coat to cover a pistol inside his waistband. . . . The South has been through much. It is going through more now in the countryside at night. But we still have the right to defend ourselves, our families and friends. Court is adjourned."

With a considering nod for all the litigants, Judge Cooper left the courtroom, followed by the bailiff.

Burdette stood up abruptly, surprised and angry. He threw Jesse a long look and strode out.

"See that?" Jesse said. "He'll think of something else next time I come to town."

"Don't let him draw you into anything," Sawyer cautioned.

"I've tried to avoid trouble, but it hasn't worked. When he gets half drunk, he's a dangerous man. He was then, though I couldn't prove it today."

"Although it was a deadlock today, I feel that we've won," Sawyer said. "The marshal was so certain he had you on the ordinance. We surprised him with our complaint. I think Judge Cooper demonstrated outstanding jurisprudence."

CHAPTER TWELVE

Uriah Webb came into the living room where his wife was knitting and went to the window, peered out at the full-moon night, turned about, and sat down across from her in a rocker.

"You're very restless tonight and with good reason for all of us," Eunice Webb said, looking up at him. "It's hard to believe, though the war's over, we still have to live in a state of fear, now from our own people . . . such as they are."

He just nodded and rocked.

"I heard what Jesse Wilder said at the meeting the other day. It was a manly speech. He understands why he's been cast out. All he asked in turn was for understanding."

Webb looked uncomfortable. "I think there is some understanding by now."

"But nobody said a word."

"He took us all by surprise."

"He and Silas Kemp offered to help, but nobody

said a word to that, either. Samuel Hill didn't. You didn't."

"Guess it was our pride. Accepting a man's help, after you've scorned him like a traitor."

"Pride mixed with shame."

He had to smile at her, this calm, still-pretty, brown-eyed little woman who in her good judgment could say so much to the point without raising her voice. She had been at his side for forty years, a city girl who had readily taken to farm life. Their only son, John Edward, had died in infancy, a wrenching loss that had drawn them even closer together. Daughter Marilyn, married to a lawyer, lived in Knoxville.

"Well, maybe, just a little," he admitted ruefully.

She put aside her bundle of knitting and regarded him without any teasing. "What can we do, Uriah, out here in the country?"

"Stay alert."

"That, at least. Why not swallow your pride and call on Jesse Wilder and Silas Kemp?"

"I've been thinking about it."

She left the matter there, feeling an impatience, but knowing her husband. Uriah Webb did not like to be pushed; it only whetted his stubborn trait.

"I believe I'll go up to bed," she said.

He rose and they exchanged light cheek kisses. "Hope you sleep well," he said.

As she started for the stairs, he caught a distant sound. It kept growing. A hard beat across the night. Horses coming fast. Firmly, yet gently, he took her arm and steered her away from the foot of the stairs and into a corner of the room.

"I hear horses," he said. "Stay right here."

Rushing back, he blew out the coal-oil lamp, then ran back and put his arm around her and waited.

"Do you think it's the riders?" she asked.

"I'm afraid so."

Even as he spoke, the drumming increased, suddenly quite near. Shots rang out. The large glass window crashed. More shots as bullets battered the house. They both flinched. He held her tighter.

She bowed her head, murmuring sadly: "Our beautiful window with the wreath of painted roses."

He had a grimmer thought, lessened with relief: *What if we'd been sitting in there as we often do in the evening to look out at the stars?*

An eerie stillness pervaded as the hoof beats faded, gone. He lit the lamp and looked around. Bullets had struck the open bookcases. He drew Eunice to her chair, patted her shoulder, and said: "I'm going out. Better see about Jack and Zeke. They'll be scared out of their wits. Can't blame them."

She looked at him with great pain and fear. "Are you sure the riders are gone?"

"Positive. They never hang around. They shoot and run."

"Don't stay long."

"I won't. It's all right now."

"I'm afraid, Uriah." She was close to weeping.

That got to him. He patted her again, and said— "I'll get us another window, with roses, if I have to haul it in myself from Knoxville."—and left her.

Striding across the moon-washed yard with lantern and loaded shotgun, he could not ignore the pointing finger of blame now for having waited so long without taking some sort of action. Like

Samuel Hill, he had put off, waited for what? For other men to do something? A wonder dear Eunice wasn't wounded or killed tonight. Thank God, she wasn't!

Nearing the cabins, he called out and two Negroes appeared at once.

"Marse Webb, you-all all right?"

That was Zeke, his oldest hand, the only one who had chosen to stay when freed. Jack, some years younger, had gone to Nashville, only to return sheepishly months later. Tired, he'd complained, of being robbed and cheated by "them high-falutin' city niggers."

They were both good hands. He paid them what he considered a fair monthly wage, realizing he was lucky to have them. True, he had been strict over the years as a slave owner. True, he had used the whip now and then, for which Eunice had always rebuked him and afterward had been upset for some time. "Uriah, why can't you just talk to them? It's so brutal and degrading. They're not horses and mules." And he had responded: "I've tried to be fair. I've warned them. But you can't put up with breaking into the smokehouse. Jim and Shep are the main ones. You can't have them rough-handling young stock." Jim and Shep had been the first to leave when freed. For all of them, he reasoned with pride, there had been plenty of milk and eggs, sweet potatoes, corn meal, bacon usually in adequate supply, some ham, fruit from the orchard, and garden stuff in season. They could make a meal on greens and cornbread. Nobody had ever gone hungry on the Webb farm. It sure beat Nashville. Zeke's wife, Mandy, was Eunice's mainstay in the kitchen. Yes, he and Eunice were lucky and thankful for the good years, and for escaping tonight's brush with death. These humbling thoughts rushed through his mind now.

"We're all right," Webb told them. "They shot into the house and shattered the front window. Daylight will show more damage. But we're lucky. I heard 'em coming, blew out the light, and then we took cover."

"Oh, Lawdy," Zeke moaned.

"How's everybody here?" Webb asked, speaking fast. "Did they shoot into the cabins?"

"No, thank de Lord. Jack, you tell Marse Webb de rest," Zeke said, cotton head bobbing. "Ah'm still shakin'. Ah kin still see dem ghos' riders."

"Well," Jack said, "ain't much to tell, suh. Dey slowed down a little, den Ah heard one say . . . 'Let's git outta here.' . . . and dey took off."

"Good. Nobody shot. Now come to the house and help me clean up the glass."

"Yassuh," Zeke said. "Ah figger de good Lord saved us all."

Soon after first light, Webb was in a buggy headed over to Samuel Hill's farm. Eunice was still fearful, but, after the wreckage of the cherished window had been cleared away, and, with Mandy staying in the house, she had calmed down enough for him to leave.

He found Hill *en route* to his barns.

"Well, we got hit last night," Webb informed him.

"The hell you say!"

"Eunice wasn't hurt, thank God, though it's a wonder. The usual maneuver . . . shot into the house and rode off fast. Shattered the front window. Eunice may go stay with her sister in Lewisburg, but is afraid to leave me. I told her that so far the riders haven't come back a second time."

"Small comfort," Hill snorted. "I know by now you're thinkin' the same way I am, or you wouldn't be here."

"I am. We've got to do something, Sam."

"Absolutely. We need experienced fighting men like Jesse Wilder and Silas Kemp. We need to get organized somehow."

"We'll have to eat humble pie, Sam, after all that's been said. I ordered Jesse off my place when he came to buy milk. Eunice was unhappy with me."

"No worse than what I said at the meeting." He looked down. "How high and righteous I must've sounded."

"Well, get in. Let's go."

"Soon as I leave word at the house."

Jesse could not contain his astonishment on hearing the rush of hoof clatter when he went to the door and saw the callers. He waited until they had climbed down from the buggy and, with hesitant steps, approached the house. Then he came out on the porch and said: "Good morning."

They stopped. Webb glanced at Hill, waiting for him to say something. But Hill, embarrassed, did not, and Webb, shamefaced, said: "Jesse, we've come to ask you and Silas to take over. With apologies from Sam and I, who have treated you. . . . Riders shot up my house last night. Missus Webb narrowly escaped injury or death. I realized then something has to be done. We need action. Military men like you and Silas. Since the meeting, I guess we've been waiting for something to happen. It did last night . . . the wrong way."

"We understand how you feel toward us," Hill said. "I sincerely apologize for what I said at the meeting. It's been heavy on my mind ever since . . . how self-righteous I sounded. Samuel Hill, who never fired a shot in the war." He shook his head. "As Uriah said, Jesse, we've come to eat humble pie, and rightly so, after spurning your help and Silas's. We hope you'll forgive us and take over."

Jesse was too stunned for words. But just then, seeing Susan at the door, he said: "Please, tell Gabe to find Silas, that Mister Webb and Mister Hill are here. I think Silas is working on his wagon." Turning to the men, he gestured to chairs. "Come up. I'll help, if I can, and if Silas will." He shook hands with each man.

No more was said during the uneasy waiting. Jesse's own feelings were untroubled. He understood these old neighbors better than they did themselves, having felt at ease ever since he had cleared his mind at the general meeting. He knew why they had treated him that way. Hell, because they were fire-eating Southerners and now, like men, they had come here today to apologize for what they had said. Yes, something must be done. *Come on, Silas.*

He arrived forthwith, yet without hurry.

Jesse waved him to the porch. "Come up, Silas. Mister Hill and Mister Webb have asked us to take over about the night riders. I said I would help, if you will. The Webb house was fired on last night. Missus Webb escaped injury, thank God."

"It was close," Webb related. "Wife and I were still up. Of a sudden I heard 'em on the run. I put out the lamp and got her to a corner. Didn't wait long. They shot out the front window, and some shots hit the living room where we'd been sitting." He shook his head in a marveling way.

"Good God!" Kemp said.

"Furthermore," Hill said earnestly, "we come, with red-faced apologies, after the shameful way I spurned Jesse and you at the meeting. We need you to get everybody organized."

"I'm with Jesse," Kemp replied. "It's a tough nut to crack. We found out here it comes down to tracking. Danged little to go on dry as it is in these here hills."

"Just that one shoe print we found with the bar across it," Jesse said. "Bar shoes are used sometimes on sore-footed horses. Silas is right. All we have to go on is tracking, so we'll need horses. We'll have to rent mounts in town."

Webb jerked up a hand. "We both have saddle horses you can have. They're gettin' on in years, like us, but durable. Sam and I used to ride considerable in our younger days. Come back with us this morning for the horses, and you can check the tracks at my place."

"Horses will be a big help," Jesse agreed, getting up. "And we'd better go armed, Silas."

"I was comin' to that right fast."

Jesse went to the doorway. "Be with you men soon as I tell the family."

Susan took the news without surprise, only concern. "Be careful," she said, and kissed him.

"I'm glad to have the horses. Now we can cover some ground."

Her look of concern still held him. "Jesse, I hate to complain. But when is it ever going to quiet down here? We may have to go to Philadelphia any day now."

"And when that day comes, we'll go," he assured her. "There'll be no puttin' off after all the evasion up there and the way you've been treated. But now country people here are afraid and we've got to help. It may come to a dead-end, but we have to try."

"I do understand that."

Another embrace and he went down the stairs, armed with the Spencer and pistol. Kemp had his Henry rifle, and they piled into the buggy.

"Can't tell you how much we appreciate this," Webb said as they headed back. "We'll pick up Sam's horse first."

"I think we need another meeting tomorrow," Hill said urgently. "There's still time. I've got a nearby neighbor who'll help me spread the word and get enough others to do the same."

"Tell 'em to come armed," Jesse said.

Hill's saddler was a rangy chestnut, still lively of manner. "Dandy needs more riding," Hill said. "It's his Kentucky connections. Fact is, he's been neglected."

"Maybe you'd better take him, Jesse," Kemp said. "All I ride anymore is wagons."

Hill brought out bridle, blanket, and saddle, and stood by while Jesse finished, saying hereafter he would brush the saddler before putting on the gear.

"I'll ride him back," Jesse said.

An eager Dandy settled into a nice running walk alongside the buggy. Jesse realized how much he'd missed having the feel of a good horse under him.

Webb had two horses, instead of one, brought up and saddled. "Silas, you take the blue-roan Morgan there. He's easy to handle. As you might know, we call him Old Blue. Hannibal, here, is feisty in the morning, but soon settles down in the running walk. I'm going with you men this time. But before we go, let's have a drink." He disappeared into the dark recesses of the barn, returned wiping hay litter from a clay jug, and held it out to them. Jesse passed it to Kemp, who didn't hesitate, took a long swallow without grimacing, nodded in appreciation, wiped it clean with a red bandanna, and handed it back.

"A leftover from the old days," Webb said. "I used to make a little sour mash."

Jesse had a good swallow, grinned, nodded, wiped, and returned it. "Why did you quit? That's mighty smooth."

"Some of my friends got to drinkin' too much here at the barn. Argued about politics. I was afraid somebody would get hurt, so I quit. Eunice was glad."

They rode past the cabins, the horse tracks easy to follow in the soft soil of the dairy farm, the bar shoe visible at times now. Then, as before, when they rode deeper into the naked hills, the trail seemed to vanish all at once.

"Well, we did spot the bar shoe back there," Jesse said, tracking his gaze all around.

In the distance several wagons traveled the pike.

"Now where did they go?" Webb pondered, looking uncomfortable in the saddle.

"I should've thought of this before. It's some miles to town through these hills. Why go the long way up and down, when there's the pike?"

"Let's take a look," Kemp urged.

They found it on the soft shoulder of the hard-surfaced pike as they rode up, a single bar-shoe print. No more.

"I doubt that we'll find another definite print from here on into town, but let's ride it out," Webb said.

They rode slowly, eyes intent, Jesse thinking that the passage of wagons and buggies could have blotted out any bar-shoe prints, and they saw not one more to the edge of town.

As they turned their mounts back, Jesse asked Webb: "What do you think now?"

"We know they take the pike back to town, so they operate out of town. That's a start." And sarcastically: "I dare say they don't represent Petersburg's finest citizens, though I understand the Klan has in some instances."

"This seems out of line for any Klan purpose to keep freed blacks in line. What do you think we should do next, Silas?"

"Close off the pike after the next attack."

"We'd have to know about it mighty fast to catch 'em."

"We'll talk about that at tomorrow's meeting," Webb said.

Jesse and Kemp, riding horseback to Samuel Hill's next morning, found a grim bunch of muttering farmers armed with shotguns, old pistols, and muzzleloaders.

Briefly Hill told them about the attack at Webb's.

"Now, I'm going to turn our meeting over to Jesse Wilder and Silas Kemp. I've apologized to Jesse and Silas for what I said the other day, and now I apologize to you for having said it. Jesse, come forward, please."

Feeling somewhat uncomfortable, Jesse crossed over to where Hill stood. He swallowed, and said: "Silas and I don't have a plan yet. But we know more than we did before Uriah Webb's house was hit. Later, on horseback, we followed the tracks from the Webb place till they faded in the hills. On a hunch, we rode to the pike and found one bar-shoe track on the edge or soft shoulder of the pike. So we know now that they take the pike back to town, instead of the hills. We eyeballed the pike for more bar-shoe tracks on into the edge of town, but didn't see one. But we know enough . . . they operate out of Petersburg."

Several men started speaking at once.

"So that's how we lost their tracks!"

"No wonder they disappeared so damn' fast!"

"I'd shore like to get a shot at 'em!"

"What can we do now, Jesse, with you and Silas?"

"Remember, Silas saw six to eight riders when they shot up our place," Jesse recalled. "All you'll get, maybe, is a shot at 'em on the run. You can't follow fast enough on foot. If you keep a horse saddled, you could, but best be careful to keep a safe distance. I say this with the hope nobody gets hit again."

"Not all of us have ridin' horses."

"A good mule would do," Jesse said, stirring some laughs.

"Then what?"

"Follow at a safe distance on the pike into town and see where they go there. Not that you could follow every man. Then head for home. Of course, that would be a great run of luck, wouldn't it? Frankly, now, I'm leery about one man takin' after this bunch. They'd shoot to kill a trailer. . . . What we're dealing with is fear. Getting people to sell out. But Silas and I are better prepared to help now. Thanks to Mister Hill and Mister Webb, we're both mounted on good saddlers, and we're armed. Come to the Wilder place at any time of night and we'll ride with you to hell and back!"

They whooped at that, topped off with a shrill Rebel yell.

Samuel Hill led the applause and everybody crowded around Jesse and Kemp, shaking hands and talking.

CHAPTER THIRTEEN

With two saddle horses posted now at the farm, additional feed was needed, so Gabe went with Kemp in his wagon for hay and sacked oats at French's Livery, while Jesse drove the family in the Doughtery for groceries.

"We'll park below the square, then load up in front of Balmer's. That should keep His Lordship from gettin' riled up," Jesse said as they left the house.

"I'd like to get a few things at Mister Hanover's store, if there's time," Mary Elizabeth ventured. "I wonder if he'll even remember me?"

"If he does and refuses to wait on you, just turn your back and walk out," Jesse told her. "Don't say anything. If he does that, I will have a few words with him."

"You will do no such thing!" Susan broke in. "We don't need any more trouble."

"Oh, I think he'll be courteous," Jesse amended. "And Susan's right."

Burdette was standing in front of the Southland Saloon as they drove by, arms folded in an exaggerated stance of importance. Jesse didn't nod. Neither did the marshal. But Jesse knew he would be watched, as usual.

They parked as planned and Jesse tied the mules. Coming back, he glanced up the street. Burdette hadn't moved. However, he was looking Jesse's way. An awareness moved Jesse to the driver's side of the wagon. Then casually, Burdette's view of him blocked by the women, he took the loaded pistol from the holster on the sideboard and tucked it well inside his waistband and walked around the wagon to join the family. Susan hadn't noticed or she would have remarked about the pistol, showing her concern. Furthermore, he wore his coat to cover it as Judge Cooper had ruled.

The boys scampered ahead until Susan called them back. "Behave yourselves now and maybe you can have something at the store."

Jimmy was eager to dicker. "Stick candy, Mama?"

"We'll see. But, first, behave yourself. Stay out of things and don't run all over the store. That's not nice."

He gave her a stiff, promising salute.

Jamie pressed in, hoping. "Orange, Mama?"

"If you're nice. Missus Balmer doesn't always have oranges. If not, we'll see about a piece of candy."

"Jamie be nice," he promised, holding his little face up for a kiss, which he got, with a pat.

"I'll hurry over to Hanover's now," Mary Elizabeth said. "I want to have enough time for a little visit with Missus Balmer."

"Good luck," Jesse said.

"I can't imagine anyone being rude to that girl," Susan said, watching her cross the street.

Going into Balmer's, behind Susan and the boys, Jesse saw Burdette still in front of the Southland. A man walked up and began talking to Burdette. Jesse hoped that would keep his old nemesis there until they could load up and leave.

They were the only customers, so Doris Balmer treated them like family. "But before there can be any shopping," she said, "I must tell you the whole town is talking about what happened in Judge Cooper's court. Was it a stand-off, Jesse?"

"You could call it that, though we considered it a victory. The marshal stomped out of court mad as a wet hen."

"Word is going around," Mrs. Balmer said, "that the marshal is about at the end of his tether. Now, I'll quit gossiping like an old woman and tend to your needs."

Before Susan's lengthy list could be filled, Mary Elizabeth came in smiling, holding several packages. "I couldn't have been treated any nicer," she announced.

Jesse stared at her. "Did you introduce yourself?"

"Well, you see, Mister Hanover wasn't in. A clerk waited on me."

Mrs. Balmer rushed to her, exclaiming: "Mary Elizabeth! I'm so glad to see you. When did you get here?"

"A few days ago. I haven't forgotten you."

"Where are you living?"

"Lexington."

"You bear a strong resemblance to your dear mother."

"Oh, thank you."

The shopping resumed, the boys got their wishes and a bit more, and presently it was time to go.

"It makes me happy to see you all again, and yet sad," Mrs. Balmer said. "Sad . . . because I realize you won't be here much longer. So many of the old families have passed on or moved. The ones I knew so well . . . gracious people. Petersburg has changed. A tough element has moved in, and there's no one to stop them. Burdette hasn't. . . . Oh, please excuse my ramblings." She was on the verge of tears.

"We'll be in again," Jesse said, and put his arm around her. "We've enjoyed seeing you today, and thank you for helping us with the shopping."

"Don't hurry. My helper will take everything out."

"I'll get the wagon."

Leaving the store with the women chatting away, he was relieved to see Burdette and the man still talking, although the marshal kept his attention fixed this way. Jesse hoped he would come no closer while the wagon was being loaded. He turned down the street, trying to hurry without appearing to.

He untied the mules, got in, freed the brake, and backed the wagon around to head up the street. Burdette and the man were still in front of the Southland. Another man left the saloon. He called to Burdette and, weaving, made for the marshal. *Another drunk*, Jesse thought. The drunk slapped Burdette on the back and started talking fast, head bobbing. *Good. Keep Burdette there.*

Jesse parked and entered the store, the upstreet scene unchanged.

"We're ready to go," Susan said.

More good-byes, then Mrs. Balmer busied herself directing the young black helper.

As they went out, followed by the loaded helper, Jesse glanced toward the saloon and gave a little jerk. Burdette wasn't there. He was striding down the other side of the street.

"What is it?" Susan asked.

"Burdette. He appears to be coming this way. There may be trouble."

"I'm glad you're around."

"Let's load and go. But don't hurry. I refuse to run." He gave the helper a hand and the man went back again before all the groceries were in the wagon. Meanwhile, Mrs. Balmer had followed them out.

Another moment and Jesse heard Burdette's challenging voice as he had known he would all along.

"Wilder! Damn you, you cost me my job! Got me fired this mawnin'! Now face me like a man!"

"Everybody go inside," Jesse urged, and took several steps and faced the street, aware that Susan was alertly shepherding everyone toward the store.

Burdette was already in the street, weaving, taut. Right hand over his pistol.

"You got yourself fired by what you've done or failed to do," Jesse replied. "You've let Petersburg get tough. You've allowed the Southland to keep the back door open on Sunday. As the officer of the law you made no attempt to stop an attempted lynching. You've hounded me again and again, figuring you'd look like a Southern patriot because I'd worn the blue out West. But I didn't ask to have you fired. Maybe I should have long before now."

"But you caused it, Wilder!"

"You brought it on yourself. Now go on. You're drunk! My family's ready to leave."

"No, by Gawd! You cost me my job! You've got to pay up, you damned blue-coat!"

He was clawing for his pistol as he finished.

Drawing a shade late, Jesse eared back the hammer and fired, amid screams from the store. Even then, the blast of his weapon sounded before he heard Burdette's. He felt no pain. He started to fire again, but held up. Burdette was clutching his right side with his left hand, yet determined to bring up his pistol for another shot.

Jesse quickly shot him again, and the marshal's bullet spurted dust just before he flopped down, cursing, clutching, as he lost his pistol.

Susan was at Jesse's side almost before he could move, reaching for him. "You all right?"

"Yes."

He walked across to the marshal, who was writhing about and still cursing him. Looking down, Jesse felt a vast disgust for the man.

Suddenly he heard excited voices as men filled the street.

"I'm glad I didn't kill him," Jesse said around, "but he sure had a hankerin' to kill me."

"He came at you, hell-bent," an older voice said. "You had to defend yourself."

"I hope that will be well understood."

"He's lucky you didn't kill him."

More voices joined in.

"Burdette's played his last card in this town!"

"Somebody get Doc Gates!"

"Where shall we take 'im now?"

"Hell, the Southland . . . where he hangs out most of the time. Here, you men. Lend a hand."

"He smells like a brewery."

Jesse didn't offer to help. He would show no crocodile concern for the man who had called him a traitor in public and twice tried to kill him. A dull anger filled him as he walked away, just now realizing how slow he'd been getting off that first shot, simply because he hadn't wanted to kill Burdette—a foolish thing, with his own life at deadly risk, and his family depending on him.

Susan was waiting by the wagon, her eyes enveloping him.

"It's all right," he said, almost matter-of-fact about it. "Burdette's going to live. But he's through as marshal. No more bluster and blow. He won't bother us again. Now let's go home."

"After we go into the store and collect ourselves."

B. L. Sawyer showed up next morning. "As your attorney, I thought I should come out and see how you're doing. I was visiting an old client south of town yesterday, so I missed the gunfight. Thank God you're all right, Jesse. I've had several witnesses tell me what happened. All agreed that Burdette started it. He's lucky you didn't kill him."

"What's his condition?"

"He's in the hospital and will recover. Meanwhile, the sheriff has sent a deputy in to replace Burdette, which would have been necessary anyway, since he'd been fired. The deputy is John Fraley, who will serve until the city council picks a new marshal."

"Burdette may still try to bushwhack me."

"I understand it will be a long time before he can draw a pistol right-handed. They say he's crippled."

"I consider that good news, to keep him at bay, until we can go to Philadelphia."

"Oh, yes," Susan said.

"I've heard nothing. But I'll write Mister Randolph again today. He strikes me as a reasonable attorney at law in the awkward position of representing a most unreasonable client."

"The sooner we hear the better," Susan said. "To avoid trouble yesterday, Jesse made a point of parking below Balmer's and picking up our groceries on the way out, and still that horrid man tried to kill him."

"But Jesse kept a cool head. Yancey Hanover, who was watching from the store, said Jesse tried to talk Burdette out of it. Nate Burdette owes his life to you, Jesse, but would never admit it. Well, I must go and see if I can stir Philadelphia."

"There goes a mighty good man," Jesse said as they watched Sawyer drive off. "If anybody can win for us in Philadelphia, that country lawyer can."

"He always makes me feel more encouraged," she said, her head resting on Jesse's shoulder.

Time dragged on all of them. Jesse, in the attic looking for books, found a treasured box of crayons that Mary Elizabeth had used in grade school. Delighted, using ledger sheets from the office, she drew funny faces for the boys, and then instructed them how to draw and color their own creations.

"Did you ever see anybody like her with kids?" Susan exclaimed to Jesse.

"Yes, you and Gabe." He laughed. "She's a natural-born teacher. This time next year our boys will be in a regular school. Right now we can say they're going to a country school."

"With a teacher who loves them."

"It helps make up for Lexington. There's a big silence up there. Not one letter from Blair."

Early that cool evening everyone gathered in the living room before the cherry-red coals of an oak fire. After a while the sudden drumbeat of running horses broke the quiet. At once Jesse darkened the room and moved the family to the wall by the fireplace.

Oddly, he thought, it didn't sound like a bunch of riders. Instead, like two or three. Kemp slipped away to his room for a rifle and Jesse had his Spencer nearby.

Instead of firing and rushing by the house, the horsemen slowed and one shouted: "Jesse Wilder.... Silas Kemp! We need help!"

Jesse started to the front door, but Kemp said: "Hold on. May be a trick to get at you."

As Jesse paused, a rider shouted: "They just shot up Jim Thatcher's place! Seriously wounded his wife!"

Hurrying out on the porch with Kemp, Jesse saw the restless shapes of two horsemen.

"Who are you?" Jesse asked.

"I'm Frank Morgan," one said. "With me is Billy Thatcher, Jim's brother."

"How badly wounded is Jim's wife?"

"She's lost a lot of blood, but they got the bleeding stopped. Thank the Lord, there's women to help. Some of her folks came to visit."

Jesse cursed under his breath. "The bastards! Silas and I are already saddled. We'd better ride for the pike. Just where is the Thatcher place?"

"This side of Samuel Hill's farm. About three miles from the pike."

"I'll be with you men in a minute." Susan had lit the lamp. Looking at the anxious faces of his family, he said: "You heard the man. Jim Thatcher's wife wounded. We're all riding for the pike, though it may be too late by now."

"Be careful," Susan said. "And good luck."

Gabe had already brought up both saddle horses. Riding under a last-quarter moon, they reached the pike and, at Jesse's suggestion, took position on one side.

"If we split up, two to a side, we might shoot into each other."

The silence grew heavy on the pike. Nothing moved.

"Them riders are already in town before now," Morgan said in a blaming tone. "We rode as fast as we could."

"There's no place for blame," Jesse reminded him. "You and Billy did the best any two men could. And remember, these thugs don't loiter along the way after they've shot into a house. They tear out for the pike."

After a long wait, they heard a single horse approaching at a leisurely trot, pulling a buggy with two giggling lovers.

"Let's stop 'em," Morgan said. "Maybe they know something."

"Go ahead," Jesse agreed.

Morgan rode out into the middle of the pike. " 'Evening, folks. Please halt."

The driver pulled up with a jerk.

"I'm Frank Morgan. We're on the lookout for riders dressed in white that shot up Jim Thatcher's place tonight and wounded the missus. Have you seen any such riders?"

"Oh, no," replied a shocked young man. "The Thatchers . . . that's awful!"

"Maybe we'd better go home, Johnny," the girl said.

"Yeah."

Johnny turned the buggy around and departed at a fast trot.

It was after midnight when the four gave up their watch and turned for home.

"I feel plumb helpless," Morgan said, still in the blaming tone. "Time a man could slap a saddle on a horse, they're long gone."

"And what could one man do?" Billy Thatcher demanded. "Besides, Jim couldn't leave Thelma."

"Out of the question. I'm sure not blamin' Jim."

"How do you see it now, Silas?" Jesse asked. "We have to give chase if we can. What else can we do?"

"Maybe we ought to work from the other end. We know this bunch rides out of Petersburg. Where do they hang out? Where do they pass the word to meet for the night's raid?"

"Then where do they meet? But, first, where is the word passed?"

"Can you think of a better place than the Southland?"

"Where else?"

They left it hanging there and shook hands on parting, all agreeing to help when needed. Morgan was still grousing to himself as he and Billy Thatcher rode off.

Jesse went on in thoughtful silence for a way, then said: "The Southland leads right back to the bunch that tried to hang Gabe. He was walking down the street when he saw Ike Cole come out the back door of the saloon, open on Sunday, mind you. Ike followed him. When Gabe ignored Ike's insults, Ike went back to the saloon for his boys. They seized Gabe and took him to a barn where they started to beat him up. When they ran out of whiskey, they got more from the Southland, gettin' ready fer the hangin'. Hell, that's it, Silas! What could be a better meeting place than the barn? I think we can find it. Gabe can help direct us. Let's go in tomorrow and see!"

"Don't forget the bar shoe."

CHAPTER FOURTEEN

Headed for town next morning, both still armed as last night, Jesse said to Kemp: "Gabe just has general recollections about the location of the barn. He was busy all the time defending himself. He knew they were going to lynch him. Had the hang rope ready. Anyway, the barn's north and east from the saloon, about two miles or so. Behind a little grove of cedars. There's a burned-out farmhouse. I think I remember that it was the old Lucas place. Poor land. After the fire, the family moved to Kentucky where they had kinfolks, but never sold out. Now let's ride out there and look it over."

"I was about to say let's drop by the Southland for a drink," Kemp said. "Might pick up something. On the other hand, we might just be invitin' more trouble."

"I agree. Burdette's still likely got a following there among the topers and the rough element. Somebody would say something I couldn't ignore."

As they reined off the road and topped a rise, the

town square came into view. Horses stood ranked in front at the Southland's long hitching rack.

"I wonder if the back door will still swing as freely on Sunday now that Burdette's gone?" Jesse speculated. "Sawyer told us the sheriff has sent in Deputy John Fraley until the city council names a new marshal. Know him?"

"Not personally. My recollection is he's regarded as a good officer."

"At least he won't make the Southland his head-quarters."

They rode at a brisk pace now, driven by a sense of urgency. Presently a grove of trees rose in the open distance. Keeping Gabe's general directions in mind, Jesse focused on the trees. In a short time they came to a surprisingly well-traveled trail from town. They exchanged meaningful looks and rode faster along it.

Looking back after a moment, Jesse said: "Silas, I think this trail starts from the Southland."

Slowing his mount, Kemp took a long look. "It shore does. Bends that way. From there they can see who's travelin' it."

The trail took them to a grove of dark cedars and through to a lofty log barn and an open corral. Not far beyond sprawled the burned-out skeleton of a farmhouse and, close by, a rock-walled well.

They dismounted and tied the horses at the corral. Eyeing the clutter of horse tracks in and out of the corral, both men saw it at the same time and exclaimed to the other: "The bar shoe!"

"We're gettin' closer, Silas. Now let's look inside that barn."

The barn was closed. They slid the heavy door wide open and stood back, staring in surprise, and walked slowly in. A long table occupied the center of the runway, on it a mass of dirty dishes and pans and glasses and bottles and a deck of cards. A long bench and stools supplied the seating. Small bones and bread scraps littered the floor. A rat scurried from a horse stall toward a scrap, saw the intruders, and hurried back.

One end of the heavy oak table was burned.

"They had to get that from the house," Kemp said. "This place is like a pigpen. Enough whiskey bottles to start a saloon."

"Ideal for a secret meeting place."

"And to get drunk and sleep it off."

They went farther in and looked all about. A lantern hung from a bracing post. In the feed bins, they found a supply of oats and ears of corn, which they reasoned had been brought in on horseback, sacked. There was no hay in the stalls. Farther on, past the table, they saw cots and tangles of dirty blankets.

"They could bed down eight or ten," Kemp figured.

"Even more than what you saw that night."

It was gloomy toward this end of the barn. They started to turn back, but paused, suddenly rooted, transfixed, staring at the rear wall of the runway, at the long white robes and hoods hanging there.

They tore over and began examining the robes.

"These look too big to roll up and stick in a saddlebag, like we suspected," Jesse said.

"I was thinkin' of white shirts." Kemp drew a robe out lengthwise. "Look at how long it is.

Must've been made from a sheet. The hood or mask is part of the robe, with big slits for the eyes."

They lingered there, looking all around, fascinated by what they had found, yet left uneasy by the discovery. It was time to go.

By now some minutes had passed since they had reached the farm, and they heard horses coming fast. By then it was too late to go to their horses as riders suddenly rode up to the doorway, blocking them from their mounts.

Jesse saw Ike Cole and three hard-faced riders. Murmuring low, he said: "Silas, better ease over to the other side of the runway."

"Wilder, what the hell you doin' here, snoopin' around my place?" Cole shouted, motioning his men in closer.

"That's news to me," Jesse replied, sensing there was no way he could talk their way out of this. "It looks as run-down as it did when the Lucas family left it years ago."

"Damn you, answer me! What're you doin' here?"

A rider flanked him on both sides now, rifles ready.

"Why, we're looking for bar-shoe tracks left the other night when robed riders shot up the family farm." Jesse knew they'd have to shoot their way out. It was obvious what else they'd found. Silas had his Henry. Jesse's Spencer was on his saddle, but he had his pistol.

Cole sent him a gold-toothed sneer. "Did you find it?"

"We did. Is it your saddler?"

"What else did you snoopers find?"

Jesse knew it was building to a head now. It had to

come. Cole saw in plain view behind them what they'd found. He was stringing this out to make Jesse sweat, gloating.

"We found your robes back there," Jesse said. "What's more, the barn is your meeting place, after you've passed word at the saloon to go on a raid. Do you know you seriously wounded Jim Thatcher's wife the other night?"

"God damn you, Wilder, you know too much! But your little wife's not here to save your hide this time! We'll finish what Burdette couldn't!"

Raging, Cole was grabbing for his pistol as he shouted and Jesse was going for his handgun. But Kemp, virtually unnoticed, shot first. A rider beside Cole jerked and reined away, bent over the saddle horn. Suddenly the other horses were rearing and shots went wild, and Cole's beginning advantage in numbers was gone. Jesse snapped off shots at Cole and the others. He heard Kemp's rifle again. A horse bolted off, its rider hanging on.

All at once the action tapered off and shut down. Everything had started and ended incredibly fast. Jesse quit firing. Powder smoke hung, bitter on his tongue. Cole's last rider, crimson staining his shirt front, slipped from his fractious mount to the ground, dropped his pistol, raised a hand in surrender as he fell and his horse took off.

Ike Cole was likewise unhorsed, face down on the ground, outstretched hand limply holding a pistol. He appeared to slump and close his eyes.

As Jesse started over there, Kemp warned: "Careful. I think he's playin' 'possum."

Jesse stopped, thinking he wanted to capture Cole alive.

"He's still got that gun!" Kemp warned, louder.

Jesse took two slow, careful steps.

Suddenly Cole's beady eyes sprang open, his hand twitched, and he fired the pistol, a split second before Kemp's Henry roared late.

Jesse felt a blinding crash. As he touched his exploding hand, he heard Kemp shout again, cursing. And then he was falling into a bottomless darkness as he had so long ago. He seemed to hear again the shouts of his comrades as they fought the Yankees hand-to-hand around the Carter House and forced them toward the Harpeth River before a deep sleep claimed him.

CHAPTER FIFTEEN

Struggling out of utter darkness toward the beckoning dim glow of a distant light, against throbbing pain and burning thirst, he thought he was back in the Yankee hospital at Nashville. Yet, strangely, without the foul odor of death and the stink of carbolic acid and the ever-present dirge of moans and shrieks.

He sensed that he was on a long, long journey, although he could not remember where he had started, which puzzled him. But it wasn't the Yankee hospital, after all, that dreadful place. For that he was thankful. There had to be a beginning because there was an end—the fight so far away. Strange that he could see the end but not the beginning. All would be well if he was just astride his faithful red horse, his battle horse, bought as a mustang in El Paso long ago. But there was no red horse. He had nothing. . . . Now and then he heard a soft, sweet voice that seemed to call his name, then, suddenly, it would fade, and he was adrift again, struggling toward the light.

All at once the light grew stronger, breaking through the murk. He heard the voice speaking his name; it seemed familiar, and, when he turned his head toward it, he found Susan.

She was weeping with relief. "Oh, Jesse, darling. Thank dear God! It's been hours since they brought you in. I've been afraid you wouldn't wake up."

"I kept seeing this faint glow of light, and sometimes I'd hear a voice. I knew if I ever reached the light, I'd be all right." He stopped, short of breath. "I did, and you were there, and the voice I heard was yours."

"Rest now."

Sudden fear smote him. "Silas?"

"He's fine."

"He was the man. Without him. . . ." He ran out of breath again. "I'd like some water."

Quickly she brought a glass of water, but paused. "I'll hurt you if I raise your head."

"Just get your arm under my shoulder a little."

She did. Pain shot through him. She held the glass to his lips and he gulped most of it. "Aw. . . ."

He fell into restful sleep, and, when he opened his eyes again, people filled the lantern-lit room. Mary Elizabeth and Susan, Kemp and Gabe, and solemn-eyed Jimmy and Jamie.

He tried to smile. The effort brought pain, but he smiled anyway. "I feel like I've been gone a long time," he said, surprised at his weak voice. "Now I'm home and alive, thanks to you, Silas, the man, and our most merciful Father, who twice now has spared the life of this humble servant." He quit, spent.

They came to his bedside, the boys in doubt until he held out a hand.

"Dear Brother Jesse," Mary Elizabeth said, and blessed him with a light kiss on the cheek.

"You're gonna be all right," Kemp assured him, taking his hand. "I'll tell you everything later. You better rest now."

"Thanks, Silas. You saved the day, you ol' Johnny Reb."

When Gabe took his hand, Jesse said: "We found the barn. Just about where you said."

"Mistuh Jesse, Ah thanks de sweet Lord you an' Mistuh Silas are safe." Gabe nearly choked up. "Evahbody's been through so much."

Jesse raised a faint grin. "Maybe it's because we're on the right side."

Gabe brightened at that. "Ah'll have co'nbread ready when evah you're hongry."

"Thanks, Gabe. Don't wait too long. I'm a little hungry now."

Bit by bit their faces began to dissolve with the fading murmur of their kind voices, and the realization swept through his mind how fortunate he was to be here with family and friends. Almost at once he drifted into a deep sleep. This time his dreaming took on more clarity—images passing in and out as if on a stage. . . . He replayed discovering the barn and the blazing gunfight and Ike Cole slyly luring him in for that last shot. . . . The red horse dashed up, head high. Yet more frustration. Jesse unable to get a bridle over the tossing head, and his horse dashed away, as if taunting him. . . . His family appeared fleetingly. In his bafflement, he couldn't keep them any longer. Still, he sensed, they were never far away, because he caught the rise and fall of their sweet voices.

Morning brought clarity and peace of mind, free of the night's frustrations. It was, he thought, despite his pain, like waking to a clear day, swept clean of storm and hail.

The first face he saw was Susan's, then Gabe's. At once Jesse felt need, and Gabe got him up, groaning, and took him a short way where he could relieve himself. Next, he had a glass of water, and another.

Gingerly Susan and Gabe changed his bandages.

"Doctor Gates was here," Susan explained. "You took a bullet high across the left side of your head. He gave you laudanum, a tincture of opium. An unlucky shot that was also lucky in one way. A few more inches. . . ."

He made a twisted face. "Matches my Franklin slash. Flat lucky at that. It's uncanny."

"My orders are to keep you quiet. I can give you more laudanum."

"I hurt, but not now. If I take it now, I'd get sleepy. Right now I'd rather have some breakfast."

"You amaze me, Jesse," she said, delighted. "Now I know you're getting better."

"I'm empty, and I'm starting to get grouchy."

"Another good sign."

Gabe was already moving. "Mistuh Jesse," he announced, "ol' Gabe's gonna fetch you some break-fus' right now!" Then he dashed out.

Susan took his hand. "You're going to be all right. I'm so thankful for all the good people and what they've done. I feel divine guidance through all this, that it's God's will you survive."

"I'm mighty thankful, too. I've had some bad dreams. But they went away. Thankful for you . . . ever'body . . . believe me."

"People have been coming by, asking about you. I've almost had to chase Gabe out. He's sleeping on a pallet in the hall where I can call him."

They sat a while in reflective silence. He dared turn his head a trifle to look at her. "There's still one more battle to fight, one more river to cross. Just as soon as I get up from here. . . ."

"Hush, now. I hear Gabe coming up the stairs. He's been keeping everything warm for you."

Flashing a triumphant smile from ear to ear, Gabe entered with a tray holding coffee pot and dishes.

Jesse grimaced as they arranged pillows behind him so he could get at the black coffee, bacon, eggs, and cornbread. He ate without pause until Gabe re-filled his cup again.

"This is trail coffee," Jesse told him. "Strong enough you could almost float a pistol in it. Just right, Gabe. Everything's mighty good. Thank you. I was raised on cornbread and biscuits."

Gabe beamed. "Yes, suh. Ah remember. Jus' the way a boy should be raised. Threw in some greens, catfish, an' squirrel. Whatevah's in bounty."

After breakfast, Mary Elizabeth and the kids

came in, the little ones still hesitant until he waved them over for pats and squeezes.

"You're looking much better," his sister said.

"They say spoiling the patient always helps. I think Susan could use some sleep."

"I'll sit with you while she rests in the other room. Someone will be with you all the time."

"More spoiling."

As the room grew quiet, he soon felt himself locked in the comfort of peaceful sleep.

Silas Kemp was his first afternoon visitor. He eyed Jesse critically while shaking his hand. "Your color's much better. You're gonna make it by the grace of God."

"And Silas Kemp," Jesse added. "Now tell me all that happened after Cole shot me."

"Well, the gunfight's the talk of the town. One of Ike Cole's gang is in jail, one is wounded and in the hospital under guard, and one is dead, along with Cole."

"I damn' near made a fatal mistake, Silas. I wanted to take Cole prisoner. Make him pay. You yelled. Suddenly he moved and fired. What then, Silas?"

"I shot Cole, then ran over to you. I pulled you over on your back. The shot knocked you out. Knew I had to ride for help. Needed Doc Gates and officer help. Two of Cole's men still about, but I didn't see 'em. I found Deputy Fraley at the city hall. He knew where Doc Gates was. Doc got in his buggy and raced out here with us. Others followed. They could hear the shooting in town. Doc wanted to take you to the hospital. I said no, here, after he'd bandaged you. What could they do in town that Susan and the rest of us couldn't do here, with care and prayer? You had us all scared, knocked out like that. . . . Susan took over. She is one brave woman."

"Have Cole's men talked?"

"Talked? They're singin' like canaries, blamin' Cole for everything. Claimed he led 'em on with promises of more money. He had a deal with that Lewisburg banker. When a farm they shot up was sold to the banker's representative, Cole got a percentage and passed on some money to his riders. They figure he kept most of it. But he was free with the whiskey. When word was passed at the Southland for a raid, they'd meet at the barn. The burned-out house discouraged buyers. When anybody inquired about the farm, Cole said he owned it."

"How many in the gang?"

"Ten at the peak. Depended on how Cole passed out the money."

"They're all liable."

"Fraley says the rest cleared town on the jump. Warrants have been issued."

"What about the banker?"

"Be hard to prove a connection with Cole dead, and, besides, what's the word of the two thugs? The banker could say Cole came to him as a local real estate agent."

"Which he was. That's all down the road now. Main thing is they're no more. What about the robes? I mean, do you think there was a link with the Klan?"

"None whatever. Cole was both mean and smart. That was his way to scare hell out of country folks to sell out, and it shore worked. Too, it pointed the finger at the Klan, not him. No, there was no connection. As word spread about the gunfight, a local Klansman made that clear to Fraley."

Jesse forced a dry grin. "In the clear. Yet I have no respect for any brand of night riders. At the attempted lynching that day, they weren't all Cole's bunch. I glimpsed a few faces I recognized from over the years . . . older local men. No one spoke up to stop it. A lynching would keep local blacks in their place, part of the Klan dogma. On the other hand, unarmed, they were wise not to go up against Cole's bunch of gun-totin' drunks."

Kemp slowly passed a hand back and forth between them.

"I know," Jesse said. "Let it alone. Let sleeping dogs lie, as the old saying goes. But lynching is so damned cruel."

A kind of understanding silence built between them until Jesse asked suddenly: "The bar shoe, Silas?"

Kemp broke into a broad grin. "It was Cole's horse . . . that big Tennessee Walker. Left front hoof. Reckon he thought more of that horse than he did people."

"That one clue led us on. Makes me feel even better. Speaking of horses, reminds me we need to return our animals."

"Gabe and I will take care of that. Now, I better let you rest or Susan will run me out of here."

"Thanks again, Silas. Nothing beats havin' an ol' Johnny Reb at your side when the shootin' starts." And when Kemp looked back at him from the doorway, Jesse grinned through his pain and passed his hand back and forth. *Let it alone.* For now, Jesse added to himself.

The rest of the day passed quietly while he dozed in and out of pain, aware of family and friends, either in the room or looking in on him from the doorway. Whenever he opened his eyes, someone was nearby. At Susan's insistence he had supper in bed. As evening moved in, insistent pain returned and she gave him laudanum. He slept brokenly through the night, but free of images. Susan was on a cot in the room.

Feeling stronger in the morning, he told Susan: "I've got to start getting up and about."

"That depends," she replied.

He backed off from her sternness. "I mean a little at a time, so I can get my strength back."

"We'll see."

He was restless throughout the morning after she had dressed his wound. Therefore, she relented, and, with Gabe at his side for support, she allowed him to go downstairs for what became a celebratory dinner. He ate heartily of the thick cornbread, sweet potatoes, ham, and peas, and Gabe's apple pie for dessert. By this time the boys had overcome their wariness of how different he looked—the left side of his face swollen, and his head swathed in turban-like bandages. They came to him in a rush.

Jamie, Susan said, had virtually gone into hiding when Jesse was brought in unconscious, until Mary Elizabeth reassured him. So Jesse gave both boys particular attention, Susan helping as he lifted them for kisses after dinner.

* * *

It was mid-afternoon when Jesse heard men's voices below, then heavy steps on the stairs. Susan, smiling, ushered in Uriah Webb and Samuel Hill.

"I told them to have a good visit, but not to stay too long, that you need your rest," she said, and left them.

Jesse sat up straighter in bed and waved them over. "Glad to see you. What's going on?"

Both stood back to consider him a critical moment before they came closer. Hill, in front, puffing a bit after the stairs, shook hands first.

"What's going on," Hill said impressively, "has already happened. You and Silas Kemp broke up Cole's gang."

"I'm here, thanks to Silas." And he related briefly what they had found at the barn and what happened soon after, when Cole and his men rode up. "Silas warned me that Cole was playin' 'possum, though on the ground, stretched out. As I approached him, he shot me. But Silas killed him before he could get off a second shot. Silas saved the day."

"Thank God."

Jesse hesitated. "How is Missus Thatcher? I've worried about her."

"Doing better now. For a while it was touch and go."

"Mighty glad to hear that. I accused Ike Cole of that just before we shot it out."

Before Hill could get in another word, Webb stepped closer, a conspirator's expression on his ruddy face. "Samuel, you're doin' all the talkin'. Let me slip this to Jesse." Reaching under his coat, he handed Jesse a dark bottle. "Brought you some tonic. Some of the last of the good stuff."

"Oh, say, I remember the drink we had at the barn. Thank you, sir."

"I didn't say anything to your missus. Some women are so opposed, and with good reason, I guess."

"Been fine if you had. I appreciate this, Mister Webb."

"It's Uriah.

The men chatted on, and Hill expressed the hope that now, with a peaceful countryside, this section of middle Tennessee could settle down and get back to farming and stock raising.

"We were just starting to recover from the war, and you could say occupation by the Union Army," Hill went on bitterly, "when the night riders started to plague us."

"Have any idea how many farmers sold out?" Jesse asked.

Hill turned to Webb. "About how many did we figure the other day?"

Webb brushed at his ginger mustache. "If we include the places north and south of Petersburg that we heard about just lately, it will come to twenty."

"Twenty!" Jesse repeated. "Ike Cole was in the money."

"So we'll start over again," Hill said hopefully, "and this time we'll make it. Yes, siree!"

They left on that optimistic note, promising to check on Jesse again, and Susan gave in to her spoiled patient and let him have a drink of the "tonic," which he had straight.

* * *

Jesse was up and about again three days later when B. L. Sawyer came out in an apparent rush.

"How are you, Jesse?"

"Couldn't be better, sir. Thank you."

"Feel fit to travel?"

Jesse cut him a knowing look. "Anytime."

Sawyer looked at Susan for confirmation.

"It's really up to Jesse," she said. "Down to one small bandage now. But knowing him. . . ."

"I'm all right," Jesse insisted. "How could I not be with the way you and everybody's waited on me?"

"We've come to a deadlock up there," Sawyer said, "although I'm not surprised after what Susan has said. Mister Randolph informs me again that his client refuses to budge. It's a legal separation, or not at all. He cites the election and how a divorce would reflect unfavorably on the candidate."

"It's in character," Susan said, chin up. "What I expected. Thank you again for trying, B.L."

"Tomorrow I want you to come in and we'll draw up affidavits by you and your son, sworn before Miss Pringle, who is a notary. You understand what you will say in the affidavits?"

She nodded. "Just the truth."

"I plan to use these as a surprise. A last resort, our last shot in the barrel. I haven't notified Mister Randolph to this effect. We'll go to Philadelphia and confront Rutherford Lattimore at his campaign headquarters downtown. I'd probably better inform Mister Randolph ahead of time, so he'll be on hand. His presence at the nerve center will speed things up and lend decorum, which no doubt will be needed."

There was a glint in Sawyer's gray eyes as he finished. The country lawyer was girding for battle, Jesse thought.

He looked at Susan. She was resolved as well. It was time. *One more battle. One more river to cross.*

CHAPTER SIXTEEN

Philadelphia. In a rush, loud, smoky, humming with trade, and not a little proud of its historic eminence.

They registered at the Colonial House in the central part of the city, Jesse and Susan with the boys, Mary Elizabeth, and Sawyer. It seemed lacking not to have Gabe along, but he had declined, citing his fear of cities.

"Ah nevah got used to New Awlins," he had recalled. "So big . . . noisy day and night. Fights in the streets. Folks rubbed. When m'sweet ol' preacher man frien' passed on, Ah was glad to head West. Afraid to go back where Ah'd run off from in Alabama. Reckon Ah'm just a country nigger, Mistuh Jesse."

"You're a freeman and you can go anywhere you please," Jesse had reminded him so sternly that Gabe had laughed at him.

"Sometimes you sound more Yankee than Reb."

"It's that we all want you to know you're welcome to come with us."

"Thank you, Mistuh Jesse."

"You understand why we're going?"

Gabe had nodded. "To free Miz Susan."

"It will be a hard, mean fight. We've got to win it."

"Good luck, suh. Ah'll git down on m'hands and knees and pray for you-all evah day."

"Thank you, Gabe. I know we'll need it."

Checking in, Jesse wondered if the hotel would have balked at lodging for Gabe. Did the City of Brotherly Love include blacks? If not, there would have been a scene.

After dinner, Sawyer headed for the office of Cyrus Randolph, while the family went to their rooms to rest, the boys with their Aunt Mary and still excited about all the sights they had seen from the train window on the long journey from Nashville.

Susan took off her hat and jacket and shoes, loosened the neck of her blouse, sat on the edge of the bed, and sighed, suddenly spent.

"I'm not only tired," she said, "I'm afraid, Jesse, now that we're here. What if Rutherford still won't agree to a divorce? Knowing him, he won't budge."

He'd never seen her look so forlorn and dejected, not even back in the Southwest on the long trail searching for Jimmy. Then she'd always shown the shining hope that all would be well. Today her eyes were shadowed pools. She brushed back a loose strand of her luxuriant light-brown hair, which she wore back, over her ears and tied at her neck, and looked down.

He sat beside her and put his arm around her, speaking in a casual way: "We'll all go to his downtown campaign headquarters. He won't expect that.

His attorney will be there when we do. B.L. will see to that. B.L. will do most of the talking."

"I don't want to go there, Jesse. I dread seeing that man again." She turned and looked up at him, so downcast. "I confess I'm afraid of Rutherford."

"You have reason to be. But he's not going to harm you or Jimmy. I'll see to that. B.L. says we all have to go there to make a show of force."

She rested her head against his shoulder. "I know. I know. I do understand. I've had the wildest thoughts lately . . . where we could go if this fails to work out. Say, Mexico or South America?"

He held her closer. "It won't help."

"I know. It's not good."

"Tell you the truth, I've had the same thoughts more than once. What about the South Pole?" They both laughed, and he said: "We've got to work it out here, face to face. We can't run."

She looked at him again, the tone of her voice changing, her eyes softening. "You've always been my tower of strength, Jesse. And again I say how I found you by chance in faraway Arizona had to be God-directed. It was meant to be."

"And you're my strength, Susan. Always there. Else I wouldn't be here. Sure-shot lady and nurse. How can a man be so lucky?"

"Because it's God's will. Because we love each other."

Kissing her, a long and tender kiss, he could feel her relaxing against him as she met his lips in her sweet, giving way.

In the darkened room, the afternoon slipped away while they lay locked in each other's arms for so long that, finally, Jesse said: "We'd better get up. B.L. will be coming back."

Sawyer looked disappointed, yet fully determined. "Mister Randolph was quite cordial, as I expected. But Rutherford Lattimore is out of town, campaigning upstate. He'll be back at headquarters day after tomorrow. Randolph promised to keep me informed if there is a change in his schedule. Only ten days until election. We had a frank talk that got nowhere, really. Yet, face to face, we had time to size each other up. I repeated our intention to file a divorce petition in superior court on the grounds of incompatibility, which is about the quietest possible way for such to reach the papers as well as how it will read to the public."

He looked at Susan, sitting by Jesse. She had listened intently to every word.

"That should allow Rutherford a way out and not damage his glossy public image," she said, and pressed her lips together.

"That's what I told Randolph. A petition in which both parties have agreed on grounds of incompatibility or irreconcilable differences. But he said no matter how the petition is worded, Lattimore will agree only to a legal separation at this time."

"What did you say then, sir?" Susan asked.

"I told him that we would see him and Lattimore at campaign headquarters the first day he's back. That we intend to present our side in person. However, I said nothing about the affidavits."

"Good. What did he say to that?"

"He replied that it would not advance our case.

He said that as a candidate his client wished to avoid personal disruptions of any sort with the election coming up."

"Any disruptions now or never," Susan affirmed.

"Now is the very time to put pressure on Lattimore," Jesse said. "Do you trust Randolph to inform you when Lattimore returns?"

"Yes, I do . . . so far," Sawyer said with a little grin. "He also said Lattimore will be at headquarters every day after tomorrow until election day." Sawyer lifted a recalling forefinger. "Another matter. Just before I left, Lattimore's aunt came in. Or should I say marched in. A rather formidable-looking Missus Maude Dwyer. When Randolph explained the situation, she said she wanted to see you right away, Susan. I tried to sidetrack her, but she insisted on knowing where we're staying, and I had to give in to her."

"That's quite all right. You had to tell her. I dread seeing Aunt Maude. She's Rutherford's mother's sister. I know about what she'll say. It's no use to dodge her. Maybe we'll learn something."

Aunt Maude arrived at ten o'clock next morning, preceded by the Colonial House manager, who rapped politely, bowed, and said: "Missus Dwyer is in the lobby and would like to see Missus Susan Lattimore, hoping it's convenient."

"Tell her to come up," Susan replied, and thanked the man, thinking at least she had the courtesy to announce herself and didn't just bull in here as she had expected.

In minutes, a louder rap this time, and Jesse

opened the door and stepped aside for Maude
Dwyer to see Susan waiting for her.

"Susan, my dear girl!" she gushed, and hurried
in, wafting the familiar scent of cucumber skin lo-
tion and elderflower soap. She hugged Susan and
bussed her cheek loudly. Susan opened to the embrace and gave her a brushing kiss on the cheek.

Aunt Maude was in her sixties, a stout, active, self-
confident woman wearing the expression today of
one on a righteous mission. Her heavy-lipped
mouth was determined, an extension of her solid
jaw line and broad nose. Her blunt gray-eyed stare,
Susan remembered, had always seemed to see right
through her. She wore a lumpy brown suit and a
boxy-shaped hat that looked proper but far from
stylish. She had acquired a liking for politics during
the long reign of her late congressman husband.
Since then, she had become active in civic affairs, often heard and seen in the forefront of issues ranging
from improvement of cobbled streets and weed-
grown parks to pressing city sanitation to maintain
a constant cleanup of horse droppings on main thor-
oughfares.

Susan had never liked Maude Dwyer. Although a
well-meaning busybody, she was pushy and a constant voice of advice on families, although she had
no children of her own. "Be patient, my dear," she
had urged again and again when Susan broke with
Rutherford over his abusing Jimmy. Finally Susan
had shut her off completely, ignoring persistent
notes and visits to the house.

"You look very well," Aunt Maude said, appraising eyes busy.

"Thank you, and you look well, too," Susan said, while thinking: *It's best to get this over with as soon as I can.* Therefore, she turned toward Jesse, saying: "Aunt Maude, I should like to present to you Mister Jesse Wilder."

"So you're the man!" Aunt Maude boomed, fixing him a cutting look, her jaw firming with her words.

"Yes," Susan countered, "the man who led a group of volunteers that rescued Jimmy from the Apaches. There was much fighting. Several men gave their lives. Jesse is a Confederate veteran who served with the Army of Tennessee from Shiloh to Franklin."

"A Reb," Aunt Maude sniffed.

Jesse bowed from the waist. "My pleasure, Missus Dwyer. Won't you please have a chair?"

"In Arizona before the rescue," Susan kept on, "he served as a scout for the U.S. cavalry at Fort Bowie on a mission into Mexico."

"Oh, a galvanized Yankee."

Jesse smiled. "You might say that, ma'am." He was not going to let her get the best of them today. "As far as I'm concerned, the War Between the States is over." He should have avoided the last, he told himself. She would pick on it, and he saw it coming as she seemed to draw back.

"You mean the Civil War," she took it up.

"In short, the war. Whatever we-all choose to call it. The Great Rebellion. The Lost Cause. It's time we all moved on from it."

"After the war," Susan spoke up proudly in his defense, "Jesse helped train President Juárez's peasant army in Mexico. They defeated the Emperor Maximilian's forces."

"Others were assisting as well," he pointed out.

Aunt Maude drilled him a critical look. "Sir, you strike me as a professional soldier, like a hired Hessian."

He was not offended. He felt amused as a smile tugged at the corners of his mouth. "Hardly a Hessian, ma'am. I went to Texas after the war and some time in a Yankee prison camp. Training the Mexicans was something to do. I returned to the States when President Juárez, over my protests, chose to execute Maximilian," he concluded, wondering if he'd said too much in his efforts to help Susan.

For a moment she seemed to evaluate what he'd said. At this, Susan said: "Jesse and I plan to marry as soon as I'm free."

Aunt Maude flung around at her accusingly. "But all this time you've been living as man and wife!"

Color shot into Susan's face. She stood quite straight. "Aunt Maude, Jesse and I love each other very much. We've been through a great deal together. At times it was hell, and our lives in great danger. Surely you know the story? How Jimmy was traveling by stage with his Uncle Tom Andrews, headed for San Diego? How Apaches attacked the stage in New Mexico, killed off all but one of the escort troopers, and Jimmy was taken captive? I was in New York when I got word. I was desperate. What could I do? But I happened to read an account in the New York *Tribune* about Jesse as the post scout at Fort Cummings, New Mexico. How, after a gun battle, he had been instrumental in gaining the release of the post commander's little son held for ransom by a gang of rogues in the mountains. The commander, also an aspiring historian and a *Tribune* correspondent, cited Jesse's training the *Juáristas*."

She was thinking fast, but Aunt Maude was listening. Susan stopped, further gathered her thoughts, and went on: "Pure luck that I should even see the story about Jesse. I felt right then as if by divine guidance I had found the name of the only man in the Southwest who could find Jimmy and bring him back to me. Rutherford couldn't go with me. He said it was a wild idea. I agreed it was, but I had to do something. So he sent J. L. Russell with me. By mere chance we located Jesse in Tucson. Again, I felt it was to be. He had just returned from Sonora as a scout on a secret mission for the U.S. Army. To make a long story short, we organized a band of volunteers and rescued Jimmy and another little boy, now our Jamie, after a running fight across the desert to Fort Bowie."

She paused again. "Rutherford was waiting in Tucson to take us back. But he didn't even look glad that Jimmy was safe. He was furious that I had gone on the mission with the volunteers. I thought he was going to strike me. Jesse stepped in . . . told Rutherford that we were staying with him . . . that he loved us and would care for us. Rutherford was even more furious. When he asked me if I was staying, I said yes, and he walked away." She looked at Aunt Maude. "There is more."

"Go on. I want to hear the entire story."

"Since then we've been living in Tucson. Rutherford has refused to agree to a divorce on the grounds of abandonment and adultery. Not that I don't have grounds. Rutherford physically abused Jimmy and struck me several times, which I thought I must endure for Jimmy's sake. I was wrong, of course. In fact, I was prepared to break away from

Rutherford when Jimmy was captured. . . . In Arizona I got nowhere about a divorce. It was delay, and more delay. Finally he ignored me completely. Then Jesse's sister, Mary Elizabeth Somerville, who lives in Lexington, Kentucky, wrote Jesse that she would give him the family farm near Petersburg, Tennessee, if he would occupy it. Well, he didn't want the farm. Our home is in Tucson. But he longed to see her. He hadn't since before the war. They agreed to meet at the farm. We all came. There we hired the old family attorney to represent us. That's the story. Thank you for hearing me out, Aunt Maude. I intend to take my plea straight to Rutherford himself."

Not the faintest hint of understanding had surfaced in Aunt Maude's face during the telling. "Your timing couldn't be worse," she said severely. "Nothing of this personal nature must mar his public image in such a close race, with the election so near. We all feel he has a strong chance of winning on the Republican ticket. Senator Hart, the incumbent, you may recall, has retired. So don't rock the boat, Susan! There must not be a whisper of scandal."

"Scandal!" Susan echoed. "All I'm asking for is a divorce on most amicable grounds . . . just mere incompatibility . . . and no division of assets. I have money my father left me. I'm not opposing Rutherford's election. He's a brilliant attorney and no doubt will draw heavy support from those favoring the railroad, coal mining, and timber trusts."

Aunt Maude shook it off with a vigorous jerk of her head. "There can be nothing even faintly controversial at this crucial time right before the election. Nothing."

"Are you suggesting that I wait until after the election?"

"I'm suggesting that you do nothing now."

"You mean delay?"

"Yes, positively, until well after the election."

"Which would mean indefinitely . . . forever . . . if Rutherford has his way. He will never agree. We'll have to go into court and fight him. He can be cruel, you know. I can testify to that. A judge will have to set me free."

Little voices outside the doorway broke the tension.

"Mary Elizabeth and the boys," Jesse said quickly, glad because this had gone on too long, even if Susan was holding her own. He went to the door.

In piled the lads, still talking, followed by Aunt Mary.

"Aunt Maude," Susan said, "this is Jesse's sister, Mary Elizabeth Somerville, and our boys. You know Jimmy. And this is Jamie. Jimmy serves as big brother."

"Me . . . big, too," Jamie broke in.

"Oh, yes," Susan agreed. "Now boys, give Aunt Maude a hug."

Both stared a moment, uncertain, then did as told and stepped back.

Aunt Maude smiled, pleased. "Thank you. That was nice. You are both fine boys. And I'm glad to meet you, Mary Elizabeth. I was just about to leave. I hadn't seen Susan in a long time."

"Thank you for coming," Susan said, going with her to the door. Aunt Maude looked at her and cautioned: "Remember, nothing before the election."

* * *

That afternoon Susan suggested they take the boys to see the Liberty Bell. Jimmy hadn't seen it, she admitted ruefully—there had been too much going on at the house then. Would Mary Elizabeth like to go?

"I'd love it," she said.

They took a six-passenger Rockaway drawn by two high-stepping bays to the pavilion near Independence Hall. A tour was under way when they arrived. Susan took Jamie's hand to assure him, and Mary Elizabeth took Jimmy's.

The tour guide, a mustached young man of proud bearing, was just getting into his spiel as they drew near and stopped. Susan looked at the boys and touched a silencing finger to her lips.

"The bell was ordered by Pennsylvania's colonial government in Seventeen Fifty-One," the guide said in a rather singsong tone, heavy with gravity. "It was cracked by a stroke of the clapper while being tested, and was twice recast. Two years later it was hung in the steeple of what is now Independence Hall." He looked around at his awed audience before continuing. "The bell was rung more than once, but the most important occasion was the first public reading of the Declaration of Independence on July Eighth, Seventeen Seventy-Six."

The watchers, smiling and proud, nodded and applauded as one.

One woman held up a questioning hand. "Sir, can you tell us when it was named the Liberty Bell?"

He made a deploring face. "Not until Eighteen Thirty-Nine." And then he smiled as if in understanding. "Seems late, doesn't it? But, at least, it was done. By the way, it was rung on George Washington's birthday in Eighteen Forty-Six."

An elderly man asked: "What does it weigh?"

"Two thousand pounds. It is three feet long."

After a few more questions, the group broke up, some lingering to consider the bell further, enclosed behind velvet ropes. A disheveled man with a bushy beard that hung to his chest was the most intent of all.

The family moved past the man for a closer view. The boys seemed fascinated.

Jimmy looked up at Jesse. "What does liberty mean, Papa?"

Jesse had to examine his answer a moment before he said: "It means to be a free man in a free country as we are. To go and live where you wish, such as we are free to live in Arizona. It means you can worship God in the church of your choice. There are other things. The main thing is that liberty means free."

"Can the bell ring?" Jamie asked Susan.

"Yes. But it is not in a church and is very old, so they don't need for it to ring any more. Churches have other bells."

Jamie smiled. "Good bell."

"Yes, a good bell."

Content, Jamie went back to looking at the good bell.

As Jesse resumed his viewing, the scene before him suddenly turned violent as the disheveled man shouted—"Hallelujah!"—tore at the ropes, and dashed for the bell, waving a hammer in his right hand.

On impulse, Jesse found himself rushing forward in protest. As he flung a rope aside, he heard warning shouts and saw the man strike the hallowed bell.

It made a dull yet mellow sound. "Hallelujah!" the attacker shouted again. He banged the bell a second time and was going to again when Jesse seized him, threw him, hard, to the floor, and grabbed the hammer, and then literally sat on the man, who was squealing and struggling, until the tour guide and others piled in around them.

"He's crazy!" a man shouted. "Some religious nut!"

"Get the police!"

They jerked the man roughly upright. He reeked. One grappler punched him in the ribs again and again. "Why'd you do that, you crazy lout?"

"I didn't hurt anybody."

"The Liberty Bell is a priceless part of American history. Where you from?"

"Ever'whur. I wander whur the voices tell me. I do what the voices tell me. Hallelujah!"

"You're deranged!"

"Let me be."

Another punch didn't seem to affect him. He showed no concern or guilt, only a vague surprise at the commotion around him. He appeared of indeterminate age, masked by the thick, dirt-streaked beard that reached midway down his ragged denim jacket like some strange growth. Torn homespun britches clung to him and his toes protruded from canvas shoes. But he was no ex-Reb, Jesse thought, just a poor, cast-off cuss who'd lost his way long ago. He felt sorry for him, even though he'd done an unpardonable thing. When the puncher made as if to strike the prisoner again, Jesse stopped him. "He's had enough, as much as he deserves it."

Two policemen ran up. They took in the situation

at a glance and handcuffed the piteous offender, who did not resist.

The tour guide told them: "He should be charged with damaging an historical treasure. He struck the bell twice with a hammer. There it is, on the floor."

"The prosecutor will have to decide on the charges. There'll be a hearing."

"Give 'im a bath first!" a man yelled.

"I'm almost afraid to look for damage," the guide said, and slowly approached the bell while the attacker, silent now and no longer struggling, was led away.

The curious crowd grew larger, held outside the rope barrier as more museum officials arrived.

The tour guide peered intently at the bell, then picked up something from the floor. At a shouted—"How bad is it?"—he faced around, smiled, and announced: "The damage is superficial, thank the Lord! The lip of the bell is dented in two places, and I found a few small chips . . . but that's all."

"Hooray! Hooray!" the crowd cheered and applauded.

"There are other dents," the guide told them. "We have to remember our grand old bell had much use and abuse in its early history. We can touch it up, and it'll look as good as before."

The crowd hung on, talking, wondering, still watching. A young man rushed up and began asking questions. Several men pointed at Jesse.

The young man hastened to Jesse. "Sir, I'm Daniel Hanna from the *Inquirer*. I understand you're the man who just stopped the attacker of our beloved Liberty Bell."

"I didn't stop him entirely. He'd already struck

the bell twice with a hammer before I could bring him down."

"But he didn't strike the bell again?"

"No. I grabbed him and took the hammer. I had plenty of help after that. Feelings were high. He might have been beaten senseless. As it was, he got punched."

"Did he say why he did it?"

"He said voices told him to."

All this time Hanna was scribbling furiously in a notebook. "Voices! He must be out of his head. Did he have another weapon on his person?"

"I saw only the hammer. I didn't search him. Neither did others or the police at that time. Didn't seem necessary. I doubt that he was otherwise armed, unless it was a pocket knife."

"How would you describe this person?"

"A homeless wanderer . . . a lost person . . . pathetic . . . in near rags."

"His age, about?"

"In his late thirties or early forties. Just a guess."

"May I have your name, sir?"

Jesse hesitated instinctively, being in Yankee country. The family was banked around him, all ears and proud, but, when he saw Susan nod, he said: "Jesse Wilder."

"Perhaps you served in the Civil War?"

"I'm an ex-Confederate. Army of Tennessee. I'm here with my family from Petersburg, Tennessee."

"May I ask your rank, sir?"

"A captain of infantry."

Hanna raised a jubilant hand. "This caps the story. A former Confederate officer saves the Liberty Bell!"

Jesse felt uncomfortable. "Mister Hanna, I believe the Liberty Bell stands for all Americans."

"Oh, yes, indeed. North and South. I didn't mean not, sir. This is just such an unusual happening. May I ask the nature of your visit here, Captain Wilder? It is most fortunate that you happened to be here to-day and acted decisively."

"We're here just to see your fair city," Jesse replied, anxious to end the interview. "We must get along now. Thank you, Mister Hanna." He shook hands and moved off, the family with him.

CHAPTER SEVENTEEN

"Mister Randolph informed me, by messenger, a short time ago that Rutherford Lattimore will be conferring with workers at his campaign headquarters all afternoon," Sawyer said. "I suggest that we leave early this afternoon, if that's convenient?"

"I see no reason to put it off," Susan said firmly. "Does Rutherford know we're coming today?"

"All he knows is that we're in town. I didn't give the messenger any indication that we're coming to see Lattimore. I was afraid Lattimore might dodge us."

"Good point," Jesse said.

"However, Randolph may expect us after that explicit message. In addition, I suggest that the entire family go. That will strengthen our purpose. Now, Susan, you and Jesse must be prepared to expect total disagreement. I expect Lattimore will demand that we delay everything until after the election."

"Oh, yes," she said. "Furthermore, and first of all,

he will be furious with us for daring to come there. I know his temper. He will be livid."

"But don't lose your temper, too. Nor you, Jesse."

"I won't, unless he tries to harm her."

"Make up your minds to rein in your anger. Also, Lattimore is the man of the moment. The favored candidate. He must show restraint as a public figure."

"But will he?" Susan differed.

"If he blows up, I would expect Mister Randolph to say the matter should be discussed in private and will suggest we adjourn to another room. And remember, you say nothing about the affidavits until after I do . . . if I do . . . and if you're asked to."

They chatted on. Jesse's role in preventing possibly devastating damage to the cherished Liberty Bell had made page one of the *Inquirer* as the lead story. A sanity hearing was scheduled for the attacker, described as a "down-and-out piteous wanderer."

"I can't think of a better way for you to hit town," Sawyer said with a smile. "And for a former Confederate officer to act so expeditiously was outstanding."

"In view of why we're here, I tried to be careful with what I said. The reporter was eager for me to say more. But I didn't bring in Susan and the boys and Mary Elizabeth. That could give Lattimore reason to say Susan was posing as my wife."

"I understand. You were wise. Also modest about it. What if that wild man had cracked it again? Or he might have struck the bell so hard it broke into two pieces. How terrible!"

"Yes. As it was, he gave it two hard licks with that hammer. After this, you hope it will be better protected, under constant guard when tour groups are going through. Yet still allowing the fairly close view we got. I admit I just stood there in awe of its history and what it stands for. I'm glad we could all see it. The boys will always remember it."

"And it took a former Confederate to save it from possible destruction and loss to the entire nation," Sawyer declared as if he had to get that in for the South.

Jesse had to smile at this good man, who had been his only friend back home after his father's death. B.L. had asked Jesse to stay in touch, and Jesse had written him when he made a radical change of location, twice into Mexico. How thankful Jesse was that he had! Now this trusted, capable friend—the "country lawyer"—was taking the lead and guiding them in Susan's fight for freedom. He had taken on a keener look in recent days, his gray-bearded face lean and arresting, giving the impression of a man in charge of himself while aware of all around him.

Sawyer left to get some rest. As the morning dragged on, Aunt Mary played games with the boys, while Jesse and Susan went for a leisurely walk, holding hands as they strolled.

"This beats just sitting," she said.

It worked for a time. But not wishing to go too far, they cut short the strolling and went back to the hotel.

"Is there anything I can do for you two?" Mary Elizabeth asked.

"Just what you're doing," Susan said. "It helps just to have you with us."

"On the other hand," Jesse said, "what can we do for you?"

"Just what you're doing, making me feel a member of the family."

"That's easy," he said, and they all had a relaxing laugh.

After dinner, they returned to their quarters and made ready to leave. Susan combed the boys' hair again.

"We're going to see Rutherford, aren't we, Mama?" Jimmy asked, looking most unhappy.

"Yes. We're going to his campaign headquarters. He's running for U.S. senator. I've told you that."

"We're going to get a divorce?"

"We want Rutherford to agree to a divorce. Mister Sawyer will see about that. A court has to grant the divorce. While we're there," she stressed, "I want you and Jamie to be very quiet."

"I'm glad Papa Jesse's going," he said worriedly. "In case Rutherford tries to hit you and me."

Jesse put his arm around the boy's shoulder. "Nobody," he said, "is going to harm Susan or you. I won't let that happen. Now, when we get there, you look out for Jamie."

"I will, Papa."

Jesse hugged him.

Sawyer arrived with briefcase in hand, his manner encouraging as usual, and they filed out to board another Rockaway, delighting the boys. Sawyer told the driver to take them to the campaign headquarters of Rutherford Lattimore on Commerce Street, near city hall.

"Second trip I've made there today," the man said. "Looks like that feller Lattimore is buildin' up a head of steam. It's hard to beat a Republican."

As they approached their destination, Susan felt

herself growing tense, filling with dread, again. She looked straight ahead, determined.

Jesse, noticing, gave her a light pat of encouragement.

They began to hear a humming excitement above the rustling traffic sounds. And soon they were there, and Susan saw a greatly enlarged likeness of her husband on a billboard and campaign slogans:

A MAN OF THE PEOPLE
HONEST AND GOD-FEARING
DEFENDER OF OUR CONSTITUTION

A bevy of happy campaign workers in colorful hats greeted them as they descended from the coach, waving, smiling, passing out buttons bearing the candidate's name and cards with his picture. Electoral bunting brightened the street and waved in the breeze. On a raised platform near the sprawling headquarters building a band of lively musicians played patriotic tunes.

Leading off, Sawyer entered first and inquired where they could find the candidate.

The greeter at the door, visibly impressed with the obviously important gray-haired gentleman and his group, said: "Just down the hall, sir, to the meeting room, where you hear all the noise. You may have to push in a little to see him. It's gettin' busier by the minute."

"We expected it to be. Thank you very much."

The greeter followed them with his eyes, thinking: *Who's that gentleman? Sounded Southern. A lawyer from one of the trusts? A dignitary from Washington? An ambassador?*

A controlled bedlam pervaded headquarters, crowded with followers leaving and entering amid an unceasing flow of high-pitched voices speaking in bursts.

In this whirlpool of urgency, Rutherford Lattimore seemed to stand above all in confident control as he chatted with avid staffers. Tall, dark-haired, handsome, commanding, patrician—the leader. Today he wore a tailored dark broadcloth suit and white shirt with a conservative cravat. His heavy beard was becomingly close-cropped.

Susan's heart sank. Rutherford had never looked more formidable. She was glad Aunt Maude wasn't here. That would be too much.

Sawyer held up, evidently scanning the room for Randolph. Susan paused, holding Jimmy's hand, Jesse beside her, Mary Elizabeth and Jamie close behind.

Then Lattimore noticed Susan. He jerked and stared hard at her, incredulous, yet, in a way, not. He abruptly broke off talking to a man and squared around, losing his smooth political face as he stepped deliberately toward her, all but ignoring Sawyer.

"How dare you come here at this time!"

"I must talk to you, Rutherford," she said earnestly, trying to keep her voice down. "We must come to an agreement."

"I'm in the late stages of my campaign. Can't you see? There is nothing to talk about."

"But there is. You know that. Can't we talk to you privately?"

"I say there is nothing to talk about. Nothing! Now get out or I'll have you thrown out!"

Sawyer spoke up in his even-toned manner. "Mister Lattimore, we do not want to disrupt your office. This will take just a few minutes in private. Is Mister Randolph here?"

As if waiting off stage, Cyrus Randolph appeared from an outer room, brushing at the last vestiges of a hurried late lunch. He inclined his head at Sawyer and the others. He lent a calming air to the bustling room, an older man of medium height in a well-cut suit and winged collar and pince-nez and a dark mustache flowing over a stylish Vandyke beard, short and pointed. His eyes seemed to project a broad understanding of the scene.

"Sorry to be a bit late," he said to Sawyer. "I told Mister Lattimore you folks might be here today."

"Thank you, counselor. We need to speak to Mister Lattimore in private so as not to disrupt the office here."

"I've already told them I have nothing to say. Nothing!" Lattimore declared, and would have turned his back and walked out of the room had Randolph not held up a staying hand.

"You should talk to these people," he said, polite but firm. "The sooner you can get back to campaigning."

Lattimore stood like stone for several counts, then nodded.

Together, they all turned to an adjoining conference room, Lattimore grudgingly. When all were inside the room, Randolph closed the door and rejoined his client, his manner calm and judicial.

"Please proceed, Mister Sawyer."

"Thank you, sir. Susan Lattimore is seeking a divorce from Mister Lattimore on friendly grounds . . . say incompatibility, which would not reflect unfavorably on Mister Lattimore's public image in any way during the election. Living in Arizona for the past year, since the rescue of her son Jimmy from Apaches, she has been unable to reach an accord by correspondence. The same has occurred since arriving recently in Petersburg, Tennessee. She seeks to petition the court on these amicable grounds, so she will be free to wed Mister Jesse Wilder and live a happy family life. In addition, she asks no division of Mister Lattimore's considerable estate."

As Sawyer finished, Lattimore sneered. "Instead of a friendly divorce, Susan should be charged with abandonment and adultery, and Wilder with alienation of affection. I'll agree to nothing at this time. Absolutely not, with the election coming up!"

His temper, Susan thought, *he's about to lose it.* Jimmy had sensed it, too, and huddled closer to her side.

"That would mean more delay," Sawyer replied in his reasonable way. "Election day is a week from tomorrow. That is more than adequate time to petition the court and get it granted."

Randolph looked at his client, waiting.

Lattimore remained rigidly defiant. "No!" he snapped, shaking his head.

"A moment, please," Sawyer interposed. "I need to confer with my people." He took Susan and Jesse aside, and said: "We'll have to fire our last shot at this time or he'll do nothing now. Susan, do you want to put this off until after the election?"

She frowned and could feel herself knotting up

with anger and mounting fear, yet accompanied by a clear clarity. She said: "The delay could go on and on. He wants to deny me happiness. He will as long as he can. I know him."

"I agree. I've been asking around and reading the papers, and all signs point to an overwhelming victory for him. With the office in his pocket, he could afford to get quite nasty in public. He could drag it on indefinitely, playing the rôle of the abandoned husband. I'm against any delay. When would it end? And with his political influence as a powerful senator, he might even win with his claims. So . . . ?"

"Fire that shot, B.L."

Sawyer walked slowly and thoughtfully back, Susan and Jesse following closely behind. Sawyer cleared his throat and began: "Since Mister Lattimore does not agree to an amicable divorce at this time in a joint petition to the court, my client regrets that she must take action on her own. Therefore, she will file a petition for divorce on the grounds of physical and mental abuse to both her and her son Jimmy. Affidavits to that effect were sworn out before a notary in Petersburg, Tennessee and are at hand today."

Both Randolph and Lattimore looked utterly shocked. For a drawn-out moment, the latter stood frozen, while he glared at Susan. He started toward her, his right hand cocked in the menacing gesture Jesse remembered from Tucson.

"You try to touch her, I'll break your damn' neck!" Jesse warned, stepping in front of her.

Lattimore slowed step, still glaring, and lowered his still fisted hand.

Randolph took him by the arm, halting him, and

looked at Sawyer as if hurt. "Counselor, you didn't tell me you had the affidavits."

"I didn't dare give away her last chance. We had hoped we wouldn't have to go this far."

"I trust these can be held up while I confer further with Mister Lattimore?"

"Yes, sir. We'll wait until five o'clock tomorrow. If no agreement is forthcoming, we'll file the affidavits next day, with the petition, and also notify the Philadelphia *Inquirer*."

"What?" shouted Randolph, near losing his aplomb. "That's underhanded."

"On the contrary, it's the hard truth. You have until five tomorrow."

They left quietly, drawing stares in the hushed meeting room, and, outside, secured a carriage to return them to the hotel. There they agreed to meet at supper and went to their rooms to rest.

"What do you think?" Susan asked once they were back in their room.

"The battle is joined. There's no way Rutherford can afford to have the affidavits aired in court and the newspaper. B.L. really took them by surprise."

"Right now Rutherford is conjuring up some maneuver to delay and get around us."

"I'd say his choices are limited . . . agree to a quiet divorce or have his past exposed in public before the election."

"He'll think of something. He can be very devious."

"How did Mister Randolph strike you?"

"Far more reputable than his client. In all honesty, I have to say I am influenced by B.L.'s impression. I think he respects Randolph as a fellow attorney."

Jesse grinned at her, glad that she could see the light side of what had become a nasty fight long ago.

The afternoon passed in a restful way. They all took naps. Sawyer joined them before supper.

"I must tell you," he said, amused at himself, "that the affidavits are in the hotel safe. I went to my room and tried to take a nap, but I kept thinking . . . what if somebody slipped in while we were at supper and took them?"

"Oh, my," Susan said, taken aback. "It even frightens me to think of it. You are the wise one, sir. Thank you. When we all came back, I told Jesse of my fear that Rutherford would think of something devious. I wouldn't put it past him to send a thief after the affidavits."

Still in mocking self-reproach, Sawyer said: "Of course. I could keep the briefcase with me at all times, like a sensible person, or leave it with you and Jesse, or hire a guard." He rolled his eyes. "This could go on and on." By now they were all smiling at his discomfort, and he said: "Perhaps we should all go to supper."

In the morning, when they met again after breakfast, Susan asked Sawyer: "Do you have faith that Mister Randolph will be in touch by five?"

"Yes, I do. Deadlines always create concerns. Will a person do this or that? An honorable attorney is guided by the wishes and best interests of his client, but, at the same time, he should weigh what is just and lawful. Sometimes, pulled both ways, the pressure is painful."

"I ask because I have no faith at all in Rutherford.

You are so wise to have put the affidavits in the safe."

Sawyer urged them all to get out a bit, while he stuck close. So, to pass the time, they strolled to a nearby park, which not only had swings but slides. Part of the afternoon was spent in a store, buying the boys new shoes and some winter clothes.

Sawyer found them soon after their return. "The message will come for me to the main desk, which I've asked to have brought here. I'm assuming one will be sent. . . . Now tell me what you've all been up to."

He's such a pleasant man, Susan thought. *His presence always encourages me. He reminds me of my father.*

"We went to a lovely park," she told him, "where the boys really enjoyed themselves. And we went shopping."

Sawyer admitted he had taken a nap and then spent time in the lobby, reading the Philadelphia newspapers. He had read that greater protection was already in place for the Liberty Bell. An armed guard now stood on constant watch during tour hours. Further examination of the bell by an art curator showed only superficial damage.

"Jesse's role was written up again. The *Inquirer* is calling him the defender of the Liberty Bell."

Jesse shook his head. "I'm thankful we just happened to be close by. Looking back, I think that individual would've beat the bell like a drum if we hadn't stopped him."

Then they waited.

A few minutes before five o'clock, there came a knock at the door. Everybody tensed. Jesse answered it.

"Message for Mister Sawyer," the clerk said.

"He's here. I'll take it."

Jesse thanked the young man, gave him a coin, and handed the sealed envelope to Sawyer, who opened it with a penknife, withdrew the sheet of paper, and read, engrossed.

"I can't say I'm surprised," Sawyer said, looking up with a weary face. "Lattimore is asking for a legal separation. Here are his exact words . . . 'In view of the election, I can agree only to a legal separation at this time. A divorce might reflect unfavorably at the polls on my candidacy.'"

"I knew it!" Susan cried. "More delay and evasion . . . same as in Arizona. I'm willing right now to go into court and file the petition on grounds of abuse. Oh, Mister Sawyer, he is so cruel. He never wants me and Jimmy to be happy. Never!" Sobbing, she sank her face in her hands.

Jesse went to her side. Jimmy and Jamie looked scared. Mary Elizabeth drew the boys to her and held them.

"I understand exactly how you feel," Sawyer said gently. "Delay until after the election would be disastrous for us. The newspapers predict a landslide victory. Would he agree to a divorce then? Why, he'll be busier than ever . . . surrounded with well-wishers and a horde of job seekers. No time for divorce matters, then. Why bother?" He looked straight at Susan, who met his gaze, as he said: "If we were forced to file later, he could go public and portray himself as the wronged husband, while he counters with the old charges against you and Jesse. But cheer up. Time is on our side, and we shall use it like a righteous sword. We ain't whupped yet, folks," he said deliberately, heavy on his Tennessee accent. "Our powder's dry. And I'll tell you why."

She regarded him hopefully, brushing at her eyes.

"I'll get off a reply to Cyrus Randolph early this very evening," he said, in a rallying voice, "informing him that if we don't get a favorable agreement by high noon tomorrow, we propose to go into court first thing the following morning, Thursday, with the affidavits." He paused and looked at Susan. "Now, is that agreeable?"

"It is. We have to keep pushing them. It's been so long now, I'd be willing to wait until after the election, except I don't trust Rutherford."

"That is my judgment." Sawyer left soon afterward to pen his reply.

Next morning after breakfast they all gathered again.

"I don't expect an immediate answer," Sawyer said. "At this hour Randolph is conferring with his client, who is seething with anger. The sword hangs high."

"What do you think they may try next?" Susan asked.

"Another delaying tactic, of course. They may ask to extend the deadline a few days, hoping to throw everything into next week. But we can't let that happen. Knowing Lattimore as I do now, I know he would never agree to anything favorable to you after the election, Susan, because he will have all the advantage. He could parry any thrust we make. By then, public opinion would be too late to hurt him at the polls."

The morning drew on. Jesse took the restless boys outdoors for a walk in their new shoes. They returned complaining that their feet hurt, but proud of their square-toed footwear and happy, each waving a sack of hard candy.

Not long after eleven o'clock, a knock sounded at the door. It seemed almost ominous by this time. Jesse took the message and gave it to Sawyer.

A slow smile played across his face as he read it. "It's from Cyrus Randolph," he said. " 'Will you kindly come to my office at five o'clock today?' he asks." Sawyer smiled, saying: "Yes, I think I can be there." Then he threw them all a hopeful look. "This is a turn, though it could be another maneuver to delay. Well, we shall see. I'll get off an immediate reply as a matter of courtesy. There is a sense of urgency here. I'll report back tonight. It may be late."

"It doesn't matter," Susan said. "We'll be waiting."

The rest of the day seemed to loiter. Mary Elizabeth read fairy tales to the boys. Jesse brought up late editions of the Philadelphia *Inquirer* and the *Press*. Lattimore was advancing to a crushing victory over his Democratic opponent, according to political pundits.

"Meanwhile," Susan cautioned, making a stern face, "don't rock the boat."

It was after nine o'clock when a rapid series of raps sent Jesse scurrying to the door.

A drawn-looking but elated Sawyer filled the opening in the doorway. "We've got an agreement," he announced. "Let's go over it and see what you think. Cyrus Randolph took me to dinner. We had a drink, followed by a long talk. As I expected, he was under pressure to look out for the candidate. Yet, I felt, not to the jeopardy of his own integrity."

"Here, sit between us," Susan suggested. "You look tired."

He gladly obliged and took a sheet of folded paper from an inner pocket of his coat, and stated: "It comes down to this . . . that you, Susan Lattimore, of Tucson, Arizona, and Rutherford Lattimore, of Philadelphia, together petition the court for a divorce on the grounds of incompatibility without hope of reconciliation. Susan Lattimore asks no division of her husband's estate. He asks nothing of hers. In parting, each litigant wishes the other Godspeed."

They all sat quite still, immersed in thought.

"How does it strike you?" Sawyer asked, a note of concern at her pause. "I don't know how grounds for a divorce could be put more civilly and free of contention."

"Oh, it sounds wonderful. I agree. Thank you!" Then an amused smile passed along her lips as she said: "But I can't believe Rutherford agreed to that part about Godspeed."

"He didn't say that. Mister Randolph added it, and I readily agreed. It sets a needed tone. He says Rutherford has agreed to all these particulars. We had him over a barrel. Bad press could ruin him right before the election. What do you think of this, Jesse?"

"I agree with Susan. And I thank you, sir. It couldn't be worded any better. Should the press get a hold of this before the election, it still would do no harm."

Sawyer stood and looked at Susan. "Then you want no changes?"

"None."

"Very well. Now Mister Randolph and I will put this in proper form and file it with the court by tomorrow afternoon."

"Do I need to be there?"

"Not necessary. Neither will the candidate."

Suddenly tears rose to her eyes. "Oh, Mister Sawyer, I can't thank you enough for all you've done. At last, I'll have peace of mind, and Jesse and I and the boys can be a free family." Impulsively she kissed his whiskery cheek and embraced him. "You've done so much," she said.

"Still that old country lawyer," he half-scoffed, then seriously, "with some mighty capable assistance and understanding from one of the best attorneys in all of Philadelphia."

CHAPTER EIGHTEEN

They all gathered in the dining room the evening after the petition was filed in the afternoon.

"I don't mean to sound unfairly impatient, but have you or Mister Randolph had any indication when the court might act on the petition?" Susan asked Sawyer.

"Right now all we know is that it's on the docket. Tomorrow is Friday, and the court closes Saturday noon. I see no chance of a ruling that soon, or Monday." He regarded her reassuringly. "But since there is no bitter fight, no claiming this and that and wrangling over those old demons money and property, I think we can expect to hear within a reasonable period . . . keeping in mind the court has other business."

"Oh, yes. Thank you."

"Cyrus Randolph knows the judge and will keep us informed. I intend to see him tomorrow."

"At this time," Jesse spoke up in a solemn voice,

"I should like to petition the court for permission to serve wine."

"Granted," Susan said.

"Needed," said Sawyer.

They all looked at Mary Elizabeth. After a teasing moment of refusal, she said suddenly: "Granted . . . it's unanimous!"

The pleasant evening seemed to end all too soon. As they prepared to say good night, a particle of Susan's long fear struggled inside her and, finally, she said: "I still don't trust Rutherford. Could he go around Mister Randolph and work on the judge to deny the petition, claiming he'd been unfairly influenced?"

Sawyer regarded her with gentle understanding. "Oh, nooo. If he tried such a stunt, Mister Randolph would be outraged, and the court would tell Rutherford to go through proper channels and file a counter petition . . . something like that. He could hurt himself before the election, because we'd go straight to the *Inquirer*. Banish the thought. Now rest easy tonight."

The tension that had gripped them so relentlessly had finally lifted, and they slept late Friday.

Susan had a thought that kept growing with anticipation. "Mary Elizabeth has been so sweet with the kids and lending her support in every way, I'd like to get her something extra nice today. A fashionable dress. Shoes."

"I'm all for it. Let's take her shopping."

"Another thing. She hasn't mentioned Blair since we left Petersburg."

"Guess she doesn't miss him."

"I think that's evident. Still, at times, I catch her looking a little pensive, though I feel that she's happy with us."

"She must feel sad because her marriage hasn't worked out. I am sorry for her. When we get back to Petersburg, we'll have to help her work out what to do with the old home place."

"You still have Silas in mind?"

"No other. And we may have to call on B.L. to get her away from Blair, without having to go through what we have."

"We must do all we can for her."

Led by Susan, the shopping developed into a near spree, once they overcame the recipient's reluctance. There followed a light gray serge traveling suit that complimented her slim figure, kid-and-cloth shoes, a stylish afternoon hat, and accessories beyond Jesse's limited know-how.

All dressed up, that afternoon, they went to a photographer's studio and posed for pictures. It took some time to accomplish, since it was difficult to get the boys to be still.

Saturday and Sunday crawled by, a time for long strolls, visits to the park for the swings and slide, games, reading, and waiting.

Sawyer left the hotel Monday morning and returned in mid-afternoon. "It's still too early," he told them. "I really didn't expect a ruling today, but, like you, I had to know. Meanwhile, Cyrus Randolph is watching."

While on a Tuesday morning stroll, the family observed only a trickle of voters going into the polling place across the street from the Colonial House. But as the afternoon wore on, Jesse and Susan, watching from benches in front of the hotel, noted that the tempo was picking up.

In the evening, after the polls had closed, the city seemed to spring alive with excitement. The family could hear horns, gunshots, music, shouts, and people parading in the streets. Steam whistles raised bedlam on the Delaware River.

Next morning Jesse and Susan, along with Sawyer, read the predicted outcome: Rutherford Lattimore was the new U.S. senator by a wide margin. Thanks to the Old Guard, the *Inquirer* reported, Lattimore had received a powerful upstate vote.

"He can thank you, Susan, for not exposing him," Sawyer said.

"Beg pardon, sir. You and Cyrus Randolph. I was ready to go with the affidavits. Mister Randolph must have twisted Rutherford's arm to make him see the light, because I know he wanted to hurt me. I'll always hate him."

"Don't waste the time. It's not good for you to hate that much, though I well understand why. Don't dwell on it."

Time seemed to mock them now. On Wednesday the family stuck close to the hotel in case Sawyer, in and out, brought news of the ruling. Jesse played bounce-the-ball with the boys in the long hallway until they tired, while Susan and Mary Elizabeth went over all the new things.

"I like your suit very much," Susan said. "It shows off your nice figure."

"Oh, my. I'm not used to such compliments. You

and Jesse are so generous. Everything is so nice."
She had thanked them again and again. "I sort of
needed something to pick me up. When we get back
home, I know I must decide about Blair. I want to be
free of him. For my own self-respect. I can't let this
go on. He has virtually ignored me for other numer-
ous connections he has elsewhere." Her voice broke
in sudden apology, her blue eyes hurting for Susan.
"I'm so sorry. I shouldn't bring my troubles up now.
We're here for you and the family. I'll say no more
about it. I'm wrong to do it. It's the wrong time."

"Jesse and I understand," Susan said, reaching
out to her. "And it's all right. You spoke from the
heart. We all love you . . . the boys. You have a wonderful way with children. We're all family. I had no
family, either, with Rutherford. It was cruel. And it
will come to pass for you as it has now for me."

Time ruled them on Thursday. Sawyer left around
ten o'clock and had not returned for his usual noon
lunch and visit with the family. In the afternoon,
they stayed together, chatting, reading the papers,
while Jimmy and Jamie played on the floor with little carved wooden horses and wagons Jesse had
discovered in a gift shop. Susan thought Mary Elizabeth looked better today. The porcelain skin of her
oval face had a lively tint. Her lips were full. The
shadows around her eyes, of late, were gone. A
mighty pretty girl. And Susan vowed to herself:
We're going to fight for her with all we have.

Hours slipped by. Where was B. L. Sawyer?
Jesse looked at Susan and his sister and shrugged.
A kind of subtle nervousness seemed to grip them

as the afternoon lengthened. Five o'clock passed. No one mentioned supper. Nobody was hungry.

By now it was nearing six o'clock, and they were thinking of going down to the dining room. But still they lingered. What was holding up their esteemed country lawyer?

Without prelude, not even footsteps in the hallway, a thunderous knock rattled the door, then a volley of knocks.

In a flash, Jesse yanked back the door and stepped clear as Sawyer rushed into the room, waving papers and calling out: "You're free, Susan! Thank God, you're free! The court has acted! Here are the papers!"

Susan shrieked and hugged Sawyer, and then everybody was hugging as they danced around in a little circle with Susan weeping her happiness and Mary Elizabeth weeping for her.

"I'd hoped the court might act today," Sawyer puffed, "so I went to Mister Randolph's office to wait. He was out on a matter, but left word for me to wait there and not leave . . . that he might be late. I went out at noon when he still hadn't come back. It was after four, and I was about ready to leave, when he came in waving the good news. He'd been held up on another case and had just come from the courthouse. . . . We both whooped and shook hands and had a little drink from his cabinet, right there. He said nothing, but I know he was a factor in getting this acted on so fast. I can't say enough for that good man."

"For both of you," Susan insisted, tears streaming.

For an instant Jesse thought she was going to faint. He took hold of her, and she looked up into his face and kissed him. In a bit they stood back, catching themselves.

"This deserves a victory dinner tonight," Jesse said, and turned to Sawyer. "Is there time to get word to Mister Randolph so we can include him and thank him?"

"I think so. I'll send word right away."

"Fine."

As Sawyer started to leave, Susan embraced him and thanked him again, saying: "We'll take a country lawyer any day."

When she turned around, Jimmy came to her, his face flushed and eyes big. "Are we divorced now, Mama?"

"Yes, we are."

"Rutherford won't hit you again?"

"No, never. Nor you, sweetheart."

After the grueling days of waiting, the joyous champagne dinner and evening seemed to have wings. Cyrus Randolph, arriving a bit late, looked elegant in cutaway coat and cutaway trousers and his handsome mustache and Vandyke and pince-nez ribbon. He spoke graciously to everyone and asked the boys their names. "I know you are both very good boys," he said, giving each a pat, and then turning to the others. "I have no grandchildren."

Susan and Jesse expressed their heartfelt thanks. "You and Mister Sawyer have made it possible for us to return to our home in Arizona as a complete family," she said.

Jesse told him of their plans for their wedding in Petersburg. "We'd like for you to speak to us all here tonight," he said to Randolph.

"As a long time member of the State Bar Association, I am pleased to say that you have been most ably represented by Mister B. L. Sawyer," Randolph began. "Looking back, I can see that we both grew up under similar conditions. B.L. born in a log cabin in middle Tennessee, myself in a log cabin many miles from here. My father was a tireless, hardscrabble farmer, yet blessed that he could read and write. My dear mother was always ready to help our neighbors and share our sometimes lean smokehouse and root cellar. B.L. and I both thirsted for knowledge, learning from simple truths demonstrated around us as we went along to be fair and give others a square deal as you would wish for yourself. . . . For that reason, I've purposely avoided public office, although I've been asked to run more than once. I thank you for inviting me here tonight. I wish you great happiness and Godspeed."

Applauding with the others, Jesse smiled to himself at what he took as an indirect reference to the candidate.

As they prepared to depart, Sawyer said: "Cyrus, I hope our plans work our for you to speak to the Tennessee Bar Association in Nashville. You will receive a formal invitation before long."

"I'll accept. While there I'd like to sample some of the fine charcoal-filtered whiskey I hear so much about. I need something for my cabinet in the office, and for an evening toddy at home."

"Already assured, counselor."

The happy evening had passed all too quickly. Soon it was good night kisses for the boys and Mary Elizabeth.

Afterward, Jesse and Susan, arms linked, seemed

to be floating on a sea of languorous light. The voices of the vibrant city gradually faded, pinched out, stilled.

"I feel so blessed," she murmured.

"All of us, many times over," he said, drawing her to him even closer.

CHAPTER NINETEEN

Now and then during the hushed ceremony in Petersburg's Cumberland Presbyterian Church, Jesse had caught indistinct sounds of movement from outside and a few low-pitched voices, proving that old battle-trained senses never left a man. And then, glory be, he and dear Susan were married at last, sealed with a kiss. Susan, radiant, blue-green eyes like pools, wearing the plain gold wedding band he'd carried in a little velvet pouch for a long time. With them, B.L. Sawyer, that fine man with great heart, who had given the bride away, and Silas Kemp, that fighting Johnny Reb of old, and dauntless Gabe and sweet Mary Elizabeth with unruly cherubs, Jimmy and Jamie, and Nancy Mason and dear Mrs. Balmer.

Suddenly it was over, and everybody crowded around, bringing hugs and handshakes and enduring goodwill, the women misty-eyed.

With all his happiness, Jesse felt a tug at leaving

staunch friends. Once again, it was time to go. The Dougherty was waiting, mules tied, the wagon packed to the sideboards for the trip to Nashville. Mary Elizabeth was going with them to her new home in Tucson. She was excited about that. As for Blair Somerville, B.L. would get matters rolling about a divorce. She said she felt her husband would agree. He was gone most of the time, anyway. She did not mean he was not a good man. He was honest with others in business. He was just errant by nature, not a family-type person. With a firm smile, B.L. assured her there would be "none of this legal separation run-around." In addition, an agreement had been drawn up in Sawyer's office whereby Silas would farm the old home place, with an option to buy. Meantime, Mary Elizabeth would help him get started; they would share the profits, which likely would be lean, if any, the first year. Silas would plant corn and wheat; in time he wanted to raise mules as the elder Wilder had done years ago, almost up to the war. Good mules always sold well, here and in the deep South. Too, Silas would look after the old house.

As they slowly strolled from the church, they drew back at the crowd awaiting them. Susan looked at Jesse, who shrugged, as surprised as she.

A thin-faced, white-haired elderly man stepped out from the gathering of townspeople. Jesse flinched inwardly. It was Yancey Hanover, whose only son John had died at Shiloh and who openly hated Jesse because he had survived the war by wearing the despised Union blue in the West.

But Hanover did not accuse him now. He seemed to be faintly smiling, akin to a gentle pleading.

Still, Jesse held back.

"I think he wants to speak to you," Sawyer whispered in his ear.

Jesse waited, still puzzled, Susan by his side.

Hanover took several steps and paused, the drooping mustache that gave him a melancholy look seemed less so now.

"Jesse Wilder," Hanover began in a gentle tone, "please listen to what I have to say. I speak for all of Petersburg and Marshall County. You know, we Southerners are often blinded by pride. After the war, it seemed that was about all we had left. . . . Jesse, you have been treated like the lowest outcast by us, a virtual pariah. Our late town marshal hounded you when you came to town, even would have shot you down, to shore up his failing reputation as an officer of the law. You could have killed Nate Burdette . . . you had that right in your self-defense, but you spared his life. . . . Thus, we have treated you, a noble soldier of the South who fought from Shiloh through bloody Franklin, where you were seriously wounded. From there you suffered the horrors of a Yankee prison camp . . . to survive it, you made a fateful decision to serve in the Union Army on the Western frontier. . . . Thus, we turned our backs on you when you returned home . . . first, after your father died, then of late with your family. But you did not forsake us. With Silas Kemp, another noble soldier of the South, you broke up the white-robed gang of night riders plaguing our countryside and killed their leader, yourself seriously wounded doing so. Thank God, you have recovered."

He seemed to search for more words, then: "And

now, Jesse, as you are about to leave us, perhaps forever, we citizens of Petersburg ask your forgiveness
and wish you and your dear family happiness from
the bottom of our hearts."

Jesse was frozen, standing at attention all during
this, too overcome to reply.

The crowd was waiting for him to say something,
still hoping, and finally, having recovered from the
shock, he went over to Yancey Hanover and held
out his hand, saying: "I thank you-all for your kind
words to me and my family. As for what's happened, I want you to know that I understand how it
came about and I bear no ill will toward anyone.
Since I understand and you understand . . . or you
wouldn't be here today . . . we have forgiven each
other and we stand together as Southerners." His
eyes were blurring and his voice was getting heavy.
"Thank all of you, and you, Mister Hanover, for
your kind words. God bless you all. Now we must
leave."

He heard a ripple of applause and warm voices as
his family gathered around him and they moved on
to the wagon. Gabe untied and took the reins while
Susan and Mary Elizabeth and the children boarded.
Sawyer and Kemp stood at the side of the Dougherty.
Jesse shook the hand of each, and told them good
bye.

"Nicely expressed, Jesse," Sawyer said. "People
will remember."

"Just right." Kemp nodded.

"I'm going to miss you two," Jesse said. Then he
climbed in beside Susan.

As Gabe spoke to the team, slapped the reins, and

they drove away, Jesse looked back and waved at the crowd of people waving at him. His people, he realized. At last, Jesse Alden Wilder had come home from the war.

ABOUT THE AUTHOR

FRED GROVE has written extensively in the broad field of Western fiction, from the Civil War and its postwar effect on the expanding West, to modern Quarter Horse racing in the Southwest. He has received the Western Writers of America Spur Award five times—for his novels *Comanche Captives* (1961) which also won the Oklahoma Writing Award at the University of Oklahoma and the Levi Strauss Golden Saddleman Award, *The Great Horse Race* (1977), and *Match Race* (1982), and for his short stories, "Comanche Woman" (1963) and "When the *Caballos* Came" (1968). His novel, *The Buffalo Runners* (1968), was chosen for a Western Heritage Award by the National Cowboy Hall of Fame, as was the short story, "Comanche Son" (1961). He also received a Distinguished Service Award from Western New Mexico University for his regional fiction on the Apache frontier, including the novels *Phantom Warrior* (1981) and *A Far Trumpet* (1985). His recent historical novel, *Bitter Trumpet* (1989), follows the bittersweet adventures of ex-Confederate Jesse Wilder training Juáristas in Mexico fighting the mercenaries of the Emperor Maximilian. *Trail of Rogues* (1993) and *Man on a Red Horse* (1998), and *Into the Far Mountains* (1999) are sequels in this frontier saga. For a number of years Grove worked on newspapers in Oklahoma and Texas as a sportswriter, straight newsman, and editor. Two of his earlier novels, *Warrior Road* (1974) and *Drums Without Warriors* (1976), focus on the brutal Osage murders during the Roaring 'Twenties, a national scandal that brought in the FBI, as does *The Years of Fear* (2002). Of Osage descent, the author grew up in Osage County, Oklahoma during the murders. It was while interviewing Oklahoma pioneers that he became interested in Western fiction. He now resides in Tucson, Arizona, with his wife, Lucile.

FRED GRUVE
THE SPRING OF VALOR

Young Daniel Wade works hard to avoid the battling militias in Missouri in 1860. On the one side are those allied with the Southern cause, and on the other, those committed to preserving the Union. When war finally comes, however, Daniel has to choose. His decision to join the Union militia estranges him from his father and the family of his sweetheart, Laurel. Now Daniel has returned home on furlough after being wounded, to find his fighting is far from over. Laurel is gone, and the entire area lives in fear, trapped in the iron grip of a gang of ruthless renegades. Will one man be able to break that grip, or will his latest fight be his last?

Dorchester Publishing Co., Inc.
P.O. Box 6640
Wayne, PA 19087-8640

___5321-7
$5.99 US/$7.99 CAN

MAX BRAND®

HAWKS AND EAGLES

Though constantly dodging bullets, Joe Good refuses to carry a gun. His weapon of choice: a supple blacksnake whip capable of splitting a hair or slicing open a wide gash of flesh with just a deft flick of his wrist. Using all the skills and cunning at his disposal, Joe plans to take out the ranchers who killed his father, one by one. But the Altons are a powerful family who own most of the land—and the men—around Fort Willow. If Joe doesn't act fast, he won't live to see his vengeance.

WILL HENRY

BLIND CAÑON

In the midst of the Alaskan gold rush, Murrah Starr holds a rich claim that should set him up for life. Trouble is, his life may be a lot shorter than he'd like. Starr is a half-breed Sioux whose only friend is a wolf dog he once freed from a trap. Angus McClennon, the head of the local miners' association, is dead set on taking Starr's claim for himself. First he spearheads a law that declares only American citizens can own a mine. Then a group of miners beat Starr and leave him for dead in the middle of the street. But Starr is just as determined as McClennon. He's determined to fight for what's his—and to stay alive while doing it!

KITT PEAK

AL SARRANTONIO

Retirement does not agree with former lieutenant Thomas Mullin. So when he receives a whiskey-stained letter detailing the disappearance of his friend's daughter Abby, he jumps on the first train to Arizona. Folks around town think Abby has gone back to the reservation where she was raised, yet the more Mullin investigates, the more suspicious he becomes. But even his agile mind and gift for deduction can't prepare him for the wild legends of the Papagos or the terrifying truth of what's really in store for Abby.

Cameron Judd

Mr. Littlejohn

With his father sent off to Leavenworth Prison, young Pennington Malone didn't have much to hold him in his tiny Kansas town anymore. So when the traveling medicine show came along with its colorful strongman, Mr. Littlejohn, he decided to sign on and head for Dodge City to seek adventure. But Penn found much more than he bargained for in Dodge, a wild town infamous for lawlessness and gunplay, where whiskey and blood both flow like water. If he wants to survive in this town, he'll have to grow up mighty fast. Or he won't grow up at all.

- -